KILLER'S KINGDOM

The outlaw King Lesley has been plundering the countryside around Henly Springs for two years. Finally, when the local sheriff leads a posse against the outlaws, Lesley's men ambush them and a massacre ensues. On a mission to rescue any survivors, Marshal Rod Delroy arrives, but Mort Wolfe intervenes, driven by desire for revenge against Lesley. Rod faces many dangers before the outlaw threat is removed and the citizens of Henly Springs can live in peace again.

Books by Greg Mitchell
in the Linford Western Library:

OUTLAW VENGEANCE
RED ROCK CROSSING

GREG MITCHELL

KILLER'S KINGDOM

Complete and Unabridged

LINFORD
Leicester

First published in Great Britain in 2007 by
Robert Hale Limited
London

First Linford Edition
published 2009
by arrangement with
Robert Hale Limited
London

British Library CIP Data

Mitchell, Greg, *1935 –*
   Killer's kingdom - - (Linford western library)
   1. Western stories.
   2. Large type books.
   I. Title II. Series
   823.9′2–dc22

   ISBN 978–1–84782–662–6

Published by
F. A. Thorpe (Publishing)
Anstey, Leicestershire

Set by Words & Graphics Ltd.
Anstey, Leicestershire
Printed and bound in Great Britain by
T. J. International Ltd., Padstow, Cornwall

This book is printed on acid-free paper

1

He lay on the flat rock, his buckskin shirt and tanned features almost blending in with the colour of the stone. Only his dark eyes, slitted against the sun's glare, moved. The morning light was spreading its brilliance across the red, mesquite-dotted plain revealing the distant roofs of the town with its smoking chimneys as early risers prepared breakfast. The dust cloud midway between his vantage point and the settlement told Yaqui George all he needed to know. The signal sent from their man in town had been correct. The posse was coming after King Lesley again.

It was more than two years since Lesley had established himself in the canyons of the nearby San Christobal mountains and plundered the surrounding countryside when the fancy took him. Now it seemed that the citizens of

Henly Springs were making a concerted effort to rid the district of its greatest plague.

However, the decision to leave the town at dawn was fatally flawed even if Sheriff Joe Henderson did not know it. King Lesley already knew that intruders were coming into his domain. The surprise upon which so much depended was non-existent.

Though he was too far from the posse to be seen, Yaqui left nothing to chance, slipping quietly from his observation post and hurrying back to a pony tethered among the rocks. Vaulting on its back he rode hard for where his boss was waiting.

Kingston James Lesley, despite his imposing name and self-bestowed title, was an insignificant little man wearing a pair of pearl-handled Colts that looked almost too big for him. He had a scruffy, tawny-coloured beard, small beady eyes that always seemed half shut against the sun's glare, and dusty clothes. But he was a great success at his chosen trade, that of bandit, extortionist and killer. He had also gathered around him a crew of hard-bitten men eager to share in the proceeds of his many crimes. They were assembled that morning, heavily armed and ready.

Ned Curtis, his right-hand man, eased his long frame away from the rock upon which he had been leaning and pointed up the canyon at the approaching rider. 'Here comes Yaqui, and he's in a hurry.'

With little regard for his horse's mouth, the half-breed yanked it to a sliding stop before his leader. 'They're coming, King,' he called. 'Could be twenty or so — I reckon they'll be here in about half an hour at the most.'

Lesley waved an arm at his assembled men. 'Get to your places — and nobody shoots till I do. We have to chew this posse up real good.'

In a few minutes not a man could be seen but they were there and waiting.

To the watchers it seemed like ages before the first rider came into the canyon. Harry Campbell had been an army scout in the recent wars against the Sioux. He rode 200 yards ahead of the posse, his unease increasing with every step his pony took. Tracks of men and horses were plain and they were fresh. To a certain degree they were to be expected as the canyon was the main entrance to the area that Lesley claimed, but Campbell felt that some of those who had made the tracks were very close. He rounded a bend in the canyon and, when he was temporarily out of sight of the others, the attack came.

A figure camouflaged with small branches reared out of concealment in some low brush swinging a long piece of ironwood as it came. Alert as he was, the ageing scout's reflexes were no longer equal to the task. The improvised club connected solidly with his head and swept him out of the saddle. No sooner had he hit the ground than another man emerged from hiding, stabbing repeatedly with a long Bowie

4

knife while the original assailant caught the startled horse, threw off his camouflage, donned the scout's hat and now bloodstained coat, and jumped into the saddle. He spurred it away from the scene while his companion dragged the body behind some rocks.

When Joe Henderson came around the corner, he saw that the horseman was further ahead than he had expected but all seemed to be well. The sheriff turned to the middle-aged man riding beside him. 'Harry don't seem to be too worried.'

Those were the last words that Henderson ever spoke.

King Lesley fired from concealment and put a rifle bullet right between his eyes. The posse was now in the trap and the outlaws closed it. Rapid, close-range fire poured in from three sides. The surprise was complete and its effect devastating. Men were smashed from saddles, horses reared over and fell backwards or collapsed as though their legs had been swept from under them. A few tried to fire back at the puffs of gunsmoke spurting from among the rocks but most wheeled their mounts and fled back the way they had come. The slaughter was unrelenting. Some threw up their arms and fell from their mounts, others slipped off quietly almost as if they had fallen asleep. Wounded men clung to saddle horns as they fled with all thoughts of fighting gone. Now only survival counted.

A few men on foot ran after those fortunate enough to remain mounted although another couple of horses crashed down before the survivors managed to get around the bend in the canyon.

'Stop shooting,' Lesley bellowed. 'Leave enough to take the message back to the others.'

* * *

Rod Delroy halted his bay horse, Duke, and his pack mule in front of the sheriff's office in the main street of Henly Springs. He dismounted, hitched the bay to the rail and knocked on the door. Nobody answered it. Puzzled, he looked about and saw people peering at him cautiously from doorways. It was then he realized that the town was strangely quiet.

A small rotund man in a grocer's white apron walked out from a nearby store. 'The sheriff's not here, mister. He could be away for a couple of days. Do you need to see him urgent?'

'I was supposed to meet him here today. I'm Rod Delroy, a US Marshal.'

The little man put out a hand. 'I'm Nathan Wilde. I guess you could say I'm the head of the town council.' As Jeff shook hands, the grocer said, 'Can I help you?'

'I'm not sure. Joe said he'd meet me here today.'

'Sheriff Henderson took a posse out this morning. They were going after King Lesley. We've had enough of him and his bandits. The council hired

Harry Campbell yesterday to scout for the posse. Do you know him?'

Delroy nodded. 'Harry and I scouted together with General Crook. That was before I got a marshal's job. I was sent here by my boss to look into the hold-up of a mail contractor and to see if King Lesley had a hand in it. The sheriff knew I was coming. I thought he would have waited.'

'Maybe he would have, but yesterday the town council told him to get off his tail and do something about Lesley if he wanted to keep his job. We had hired a good scout for him and with plenty of volunteers he had no excuse for delaying. Some of the best men in town are riding with him today.'

Delroy was well acquainted with Harry Campbell and the man had been a good scout, but age was catching up with him and, as his ability slipped, he was living on his reputation.

The marshal knew that he could do little until Henderson's return, so, after getting directions to the town's only hotel and the livery stable, he set out to arrange accommodation for himself and his animals. He had barely walked fifty yards when there was the clatter of hoofs at the end of the street.

A riderless horse came cantering down the street with eyes rolling fearfully and lathered with sweat. It slowed its pace when it saw the other horse and trotted up to Delroy's mount. Half a broken rein still swung from the bit on one side and the other seemed to be gone completely. The lawman spoke quietly to the animal and it allowed him to catch it by the bridle. The blanket had slipped halfway from under the saddle but enough of it showed to reveal a large patch of blood. More of it had dried upon the worn leather.

An elderly woman appeared at the door of a bakery, saw the horse and gasped in a horrified voice, 'That's Edgar Bowman's horse. He went out with the posse this morning.'

'Looks like they might have struck

trouble,' Delroy said. 'How many were in the posse?'

By now a crowd was starting to gather. 'There were eighteen of them,' a townsman said in a worried voice. 'They were more than a match for Lesley's gang.'

'I sure hope so,' Delroy told him, 'because I'm going out there to find out. I'll need a few volunteers.'

2

People were still flocking around Delroy when another riderless horse trotted into town. This one had a bullet wound in its neck. There could be no doubt: the posse had struck serious trouble.

'We'll need a wagon,' Delroy told the assembly. 'There are sure to be wounded men. Can anyone loan one?'

Ike Kopper, the livery-stable proprietor volunteered to provide a wagon and team and hurried off to organize it. He also undertook to recruit a few more men, although he doubted he could get helpers of a similar quality to the posse members.

'Is there a doctor here?'

'Not now,' a middle-aged woman announced. 'King Lesley's men killed him two weeks ago.'

'I'll go.' A soft female voice came from the back of the crowd. People turned and made way for a beautiful girl with long dark hair who was making her way between them. Despite her obvious femininity and youth there was something commanding about her presence. 'I'm Rose Allen,' she announced. 'My father was the doctor. I often helped him. I might be able to help. I'll get my father's bag and ride in the wagon with Mr Kopper.'

'That might not be a good idea, miss,' the marshal told her. 'There could be trouble out where the posse went.'

A determined look came to her striking blue eyes. 'If there is, I'll be needed all the more. The quicker wounded men get attention, the better are their chances of survival.'

She was right and the lawman raised no further objections.

Now comes the hard bit, Delroy told himself. He looked around. 'I need a few men with horses and guns. I believe Mr Kopper is rounding up a few but we need all we can get.'

A sharp-faced young woman snapped disdainfully, 'Why would you need them? All our best men, horses and guns went out with the posse. By now they'll have settled King Lesley's hash. There might be some wounded, but Lesley's thieving polecats will be on the run.'

The lawman was in no mood for diplomacy. 'Lady, did it ever occur to you that your posse might have lost this fight?'

There were murmurs of disbelief and looks of doubt crossed a few faces. Until then many had not considered the possibility that their posse could have failed in its mission.

'Can somebody look after these horses?' Delroy asked. 'That black one has a wound that needs looking at.'

An extremely worried, plump little woman came forward and took the broken rein of the first animal. 'This is my husband's horse,' she said, as she fought back tears. 'I'll take him. Please God, Edgar will need him again.'

An elderly man who walked with a stick claimed the black horse. 'I'll look after him and try to patch him up. I know his owner. He'll be looking for him later.'

Let's hope he does, Delroy said to himself.

Another citizen volunteered to take the pack mule to the sheriff's corral and place the pack inside the office. Wilde, the storekeeper, had a spare set of keys.

The wagon came clattering up with Rose Allen, her face shielded by a wide-brimmed hat, on the seat beside the driver. A boy in his mid-teens rode beside it on a mule, clutching a single-shot Rettlington carbine. An elderly farming type rode behind him on a workhorse. He had a double-barrelled shotgun. Another middle-aged rider had an ancient Colt Dragoon revolver stuck in his belt and an old Civil War rifled musket across his saddle, A young man, who later proved to be a bank clerk, sat awkwardly on a borrowed horse with the butt of a small

14

revolver showing under his open coat.

The most promising volunteer was a lean young man in the clothes of a cowhand. He was well mounted, had a Winchester repeater in a leather loop on his saddle horn, and looked as though he could use the stag-horn-butted Colt on his hip. He introduced himself as Frank Crowley. He explained that he had intended to join the posse but had overslept because of a heavy night in the saloon. His bloodshot eyes and the careful way he moved indicated that he was still suffering the alcoholic after effects.

The last volunteer was a down-at-heel young man sadly in need of both a shave and a haircut. He gave his name as Morton Wolfe and explained that he had been picking up a few days work at the stable. He had a six-shooter and bestrode a long-backed roan borrowed from his employer.

'I'd hate to be relying on that shaky no-account,' a voice from the crowd proclaimed.

Wolfe pretended that he had not heard, but the marshal came to his defence. 'I'm pleased to have any man with enough guts to volunteer.' He looked in the general direction of the speaker. 'Perhaps some others might like to come along instead of bad-mouthing those who are prepared to help.'

There were no more adverse comments.

Duke had already covered many miles that day, but Delroy knew that, tired as he was, he was still better than any replacement he was likely to get in Henly Springs. The lawman mounted and turned his horse's head toward the wall of mountains on the western horizon. As he did so, he saw a puff of white smoke appear from the chimney of the small restaurant opposite. Some-one was preparing lunch, he told himself and suddenly remembered how hungry he was. But such things would have to wait.

Trying hard to conceal his anxiety,

Delroy led his relief force out of town. Unlike the majority of the townspeople he was not expecting a happy outcome. He eased his horse back and came in beside Wolfe. 'You don't seem to have a lot of friends in Henly Springs,' he observed. 'Is there something I don't know about?'

Wolfe's face twisted in a humourless smile. 'A lot of folks back there think I'm a drunk because my hands shake sometimes. I have to do odd jobs to make a bit of money. But I don't drink, because I can't afford to. I'm not here today because of any loyalty to this town; King Lesley is behind my troubles. Two years ago I had a wife and a ranch. Lesley murdered my wife, almost killed me and destroyed the ranch. What he left the banks took when I could not pay my mortgage. Since then I have devoted the few resources I have left to fighting that murdering sonofabitch any way that I can. Sheriff Henderson's posse did not want me because the folks around

17

Henly Springs see me as a no-account drifter. Only Kopper loaned me a horse, or I wouldn't be with you now.'

'I think you are very lucky you did not go with Henderson's posse.'

Three miles from town they found the first sign of a posse member. What looked like an untidy bundle of clothing on the trail turned out to be a dead man. He had been shot in several places.

Fred Hyles, the boy on the mule, went pale as he saw his first dead man. Marvin Dexter, the bank clerk also lost his usual ruddy complexion. Herman Veile, the Civil War veteran, looked down at the corpse casually. 'That's Edgar Bowman. Looks like his luck ran out.'

Delroy remembered the riderless horse and the worried lady back in town.

Rose climbed down from the wagon and confirmed that the man was dead. 'Will someone help me get him into the wagon?' she asked.

'Sorry, Miss Allen,' Delroy replied. 'We need to concentrate on finding any living ones now. We can pick him up on the way back. There could be wounded men up ahead of us.'

A mile further on they sighted the distant figure of a man on foot. He was staggering when they first saw him and flopped to a sitting position on the ground as they approached. When they reached him, he was in a sorry state, exhausted, shocked and badly affected by the heat.

Rose hurried to him with a canteen of water and held it to the man's parched lips. She knew him. 'Mr Woodford,' she asked, 'where are the others?'

'Dead mostly — it was awful. We had no warning . . . Damn scout led us straight into a trap and we were fired on from all directions.' He took another swallow of water and continued, 'My horse was hit, but it lived long enough to carry me clear of the ambush.'

'Are you wounded?' Rose asked.

'No — just scared half to death. I left three wounded men back along the trail; I was going for help. We have to go back to them.' He thought for a while and added ominously, 'That's if Lesley's men have not followed us and already killed them.'

They helped him into the wagon and Kopper, the driver, looked about him anxiously as he urged the team along the badly rutted trail. Though still short of the frowning mountains, all were acutely aware that the rough country could easily conceal an ambush.

Wolfe, the drifter, urged his mount up beside Delroy's. 'Lesley and his men could be using those wounded men as bait in a trap,' he said 'They might be waiting for us up ahead.'

'You could be right,' the marshal agreed. 'I was thinking the same myself. I reckon I'll scout ahead a bit.'

'I'll come with you.'

'It's better that you don't,' Delroy told him. 'Ride about a hundred yards behind me. If you keep me in sight and keep the others in sight, you can warn the posse if anything happens to me.'

Henderson's posse had left a clear track so the marshal had no trouble in knowing where to look. Ahead, he could see the mouth of a canyon that emerged from the barren hills and craggy heights of the territory that King Lesley claimed. His unease grew as he realized that he would soon be in range of riflemen on the high ground. Then he saw the wounded men.

They were lying together in the slight shade of a couple of Joshua trees and one waved frantically when he saw the horseman.

Hatless, with torn clothing covered in blood and dust, the trio made a sorry sight although, to Delroy's relief, all were conscious, though in varying degrees. In a dazed, semi-coherent speech one man tried to say what had happened, but the marshal cut him off. 'Don't worry about it now. Help's on its way. Do you know of any other survivors?'

21

'We're the only ones got out alive,' the man croaked through parched lips. He was cradling what looked like a broken right arm. 'We heard shooting not long after we got out. They were either shooting other wounded men, or maybe it was horses . . . we didn't have a chance. Damn scout led us straight into it — saw him myself. He must have ridden past most of Lesley's men and never saw one. Either that, or he was in cahoots with them.'

* * *

Kopper shook the wagon team into a trot when he saw the group ahead. 'The marshal's found someone,' he said to Rose.

'There are only three there,' the girl said in dismay. 'Surely there were other survivors? There must be more.'

But there were not. Within minutes of reaching the wounded men, the rescuers knew that their sheriff and a dozen fellow citizens had been killed.

The worst-hit of the survivors was a young man named Fred Gollin. A bullet had broken a couple of his ribs and another had shattered his shoulder. Only the fear of Lesley's men had carried him over the distance of the retreat. His eyes were glassy and he was shivering with the onset of shock.

Franz Koertz, who had been the town blacksmith, had a head wound and was mumbling incoherently in German.

Rose set to work cleaning and bandaging wounds while some of the men carried her patients into the wagon as she finished with them.

The marshal collected Crowley, Veile and Wolfe. 'We'll go a bit closer to the mouth of the canyon and stand guard,' he told Rose. 'As soon as you can get those men in the wagon, start back for Henly Springs. You can bet those killers are watching every move we make and might even be moving up to attack us. We'll follow on when we know you are safely away.' Turning to the other riders, he said, 'You are the last line of defence and must protect the wagon. Don't leave it until you're safely back in town.'

The farmer, whose name was Bishop, looked relieved. He already had the distinct impression that he would need more than a shotgun if a real fight started.

Wolfe nudged his mount over beside Delroy. He had appropriated a carbine that one of the wounded men had been using to aid his walking. Staring up at the red rock walls towering above him, he muttered, 'I'm sure those murdering coyotes are watching our every move, I hope none of them has a buffalo rifle.'

'Keep wide apart and keep moving,' Delroy told his men. 'No sense in giving them an easy target.'

Crowley and Veile were also apprehensively watching the rim rock and the canyon's mouth, each silently cursing the time it took to attend to the wounded. The sooner the wagon left, the sooner they could get away from the menacing cliffs and the canyon, its mouth spread like some ravenous monster. From one place or both, they were expecting trouble.

Minutes dragged like hours until the wagon clattered away leaving a plume of red dust in its wake. The men left behind heaved a sight of relief to see the wounded safely away. Crowley turned his mount as if to follow the wagon and its outriders but the marshal called to him. 'Wait a while, Frank. Let the wagon get a good start. We need to be a buffer between them and Lesley's men.'

Crowley turned about, secretly thankful that in his present state he was away from the dust and the noisy rattle of the wagon. One day, he promised himself, he would give up drinking, or at least try a better brand.

It could have been five minutes later when Veile suddenly pointed to the rim rock. 'Look up there,' he called in alarm.

Men were appearing on the edge of the cliff and the sun was glinting on steel.

'Drop back another hundred yards just to make us smaller targets and take us out of carbine range. Then stop again,' Delroy ordered.

The horsemen wheeled about and cantered back to longer range. Then the marshal threw up his hand and halted the retreat. They could see the distant figures hurrying away from the canyon's rim. The urgency of their movements boded ill for those on the plain below. Quickly Delroy looked around for a place to fend off the attack that he guessed was coming. The wagon and its vulnerable passengers still did not have a long enough start.

3

King Lesley looked down from his vantage point on the rim rock and gave a low, mirthless chuckle. 'Look at them,' he sneered. 'They ain't so brave now. I don't see any of that bunch too keen to trespass on my kingdom.' He called to the villainous-looking man sporting two revolvers who was standing behind him. 'Ned, take a few men and run them back to town. Kill a couple if you get close enough — they won't fight. All their best men are dead down there in the canyon. Keep the scare into them. They have to learn not to tangle with me. I want that town good and scared so they won't try any more tricks like that last one.'

Ned Curtis hurried away to the horses after selecting four other men to follow him. He had chosen tough men and reasoned that he did not need many to rout a bunch of dudes from town.

On the flats below, Delroy rode about talking to his men and trying to assess how they would handle any likely attacks by Lesley's gunslingers. Crowley seemed the type who would stand, probably because he lacked the sense to be frightened; Veile had been through a war and gave the impression that he would not run, even if he did not relish the prospect of fighting. Wolfe was the worry. His face was pale and his hands were trembling. He ran his tongue nervously over dry lips and said to the marshal, 'That wagon must have a long enough start by now. Don't you think we should be moving?'

'We need to hang around for a while longer yet. I don't want to be here one second longer than I need to be, but we can't have Lesley's men running down the wagon. There's an arroyo about half a mile back. It might be an idea if we go back there and take up a position where there's a bit of cover. Remember, if we are attacked, we make a stand there. Keep an eye out while I tell the others just in case we have to run for it and get separated.'

They turned their horses and rode back slowly with many nervous glances over shoulders. The arroyo was getting closer when the mounts picked up the sound of the approaching horses. Looking back, they saw a dust cloud approaching.

'Head for the arroyo,' Delroy ordered. He called to Veile who was the only one without a repeating rifle. 'Will you take the horses and get them under cover?'

The veteran shouted his agreement as he urged his ancient grey mare into a lumbering gallop. Behind them they could hear the thunder of the approaching bandits' horses.

When they reached the gully, the marshal jumped his horse down into it, drew his carbine from the saddle and tossed his reins to Viele. Crowley and Wolfe did likewise although the latter appeared hesitant in his movements.

For a couple of seconds he stood as though uncertain as to what he was really doing there and then took up a position, screened by a mesquite bush, with his rifle over the edge of the bank.

Five horsemen burst into view, yelling and brandishing guns. Too late they realized that their quarry had not emerged from the arroyo. Even as they hauled back on their reins, Delroy fired.

Curtis, the leading rider was smashed back over his mount's rump, his six-shooter spinning from his grasp. The others fired then and the man immediately behind him, doubled over and lost a stirrup. As his horse swung away from the gunfire, he toppled from his saddle and rolled into the arroyo. Crowley fired another shot into the stricken man before switching his attention back to the others.

Wolfe stood a moment, his cheek hard against the rifle butt as he watched a rider on a big bay horse looming up in his sights. Then he squeezed the trigger and the rider was out of his saddle in a sprawl of arms and legs — raising dust as he hit the ground. Too late, the attackers found that they were not up against a group of easily frightened shopkeepers unfamiliar with weapons.

The remaining pair had been partially screened by their comrades but now that protection was gone and they wheeled about. Their single motivation now was to get away But only one escaped and that was because the three riflemen had unknowingly concentrated on the one man. He was spilled from his saddle as the horse bolted back toward the canyon.

'Anyone hurt?' Delroy called.

The others answered in the negative so he set about examining the bodies of the fallen gunmen. None showed any signs of life and were sprawled in the awkward postures of those who had died suddenly and violently. He would need to work fast, as he feared that Lesley's men would return with reinforcements.

Two of the attackers' horses were a short distance away entangled in their reins and Crowley took charge of these.

Wolfe was still shaking when he came to assist the marshal who was searching the dead outlaws.

Delroy recognized one man immediately. 'That's Sol Maynard. He's been wanted for years. I wondered what had happened to that mean sonofabitch.' A search of the dead man's pockets revealed a few dollars and a watch that bore someone else's name, obviously stolen. He removed the man's gunbelt and retrieved the Remington revolver lying nearby. 'This might come in handy, helping re-arm the town.'

Hastily pencilling notes in a small book, he knotted the contents of the pockets in their former owner's bandanna and moved on to the next corpse.

There was no clue to the second man's identity. He wore a late-model Colt in a reasonably new holster. Delroy unbuckled the belt and called to

Veile. 'Here's a new six-shooter for you. It took guts to come out here with the old guns you have, so you may as well get some payment for your services.'

Veile accepted the weapon gratefully, as he had been only too conscious of the limitations of his outdated guns. 'I hope I never have to use it, but thanks.'

As before, the marshal recorded the details and continued his work. Crowley had brought in the captured horses. He was eager to keep a nice sorrel mare but Delroy had other ideas. 'That horse is too easy to recognize. It might bring a bit of trouble down on you from that dead man's friends and could well be stolen. You don't want to be lynched somewhere as a horsethief. I'll keep it in town and if nobody turns up to claim it and we get rid of Lesley, she's yours.'

The cowhand did not like the decision but was not in a position to argue. A Winchester carbine hung in a saddle scabbard on the horse and Wolfe asked if he might have it. He had borrowed the weapon he was currently carrying. The marshal had no objections because he was sure that it would be put to good use if Lesley carried the fight to Henly Springs.

'Do you reckon the wagon has had enough start?' Wolfe asked. He was plainly ill at ease and kept glancing back at the distant canyon as if expecting a horde of outlaws to erupt from it.

'I think it's time to go now,' Delroy told them. 'Lesley might come after us again if he has enough men. We'll have to leave these bodies where they are.'

'Aren't you worried they'll poison the buzzards,' Crowley remarked, as he took the reins of the captured horses.

Veile was riding beside Delroy. 'How are we going to tell folks about this? Half the town lost relatives here today.' He shook his head as though in disbelief. 'There's never been a disaster like this at Henly Springs.'

'There could be another one,' the lawman reminded him, 'if half the stories about the size of Lesley's gang are true. We hurt him here and for the sake of his reputation, he's sure to hit back.'

'He wouldn't dare attack the town, would he?'

'I would if I were him. Men like Lesley survive because people are terrified of them. He has to teach people that they cannot win if they oppose him.'

They caught up with the wagon just before it reached Henly Springs. Delroy and his men had faced a barrage of questions from the others.

'We heard all the shooting.' Fred Hyles said. 'Miss Allen wanted us to go back and help — she called us a few nasty names when we wouldn't. Dexter and I figured that our main job was to stay with the wagon. We had four hurt men and a lady to protect. Was that right?'

'You did right. This town's going to need every gun it has before this is over. I'll explain that to Miss Allen if she's still mad at you.' As he spoke, Delroy took a small revolver from his belt. It was a Navy Colt with a shortened barrel that had been converted to take .38 cartridges. He passed the weapon to the boy. 'One of the bandits was carrying this as a hideout gun. You'd better take it. If you're staying with me you'll need more than a single-shot rifle. Be careful — it's loaded.'

Eagerly the boy took the weapon, admired it for a second and put it in the side pocket of his coat. 'I'll stay with you, Marshal,' he promised.

People were crowding into the town's single street as they saw the posse returning with the wagon. Uneasy muttering broke out as it was realized that none of the original posse members could be seen.

'Is that all?' a young woman called in a despairing voice. 'Where's my husband — Arthur Mason?'

Kopper, as a long-time resident of the town, had been dreading this moment. He hauled the team to a stop. 'We have wounded men in the back,' he called. 'We saved all who could be saved, but most of them are still out there . . . '

There was a rush to lower the tailboard of the wagon and moans of anguish and despair from those with missing loved ones.

Rose, fighting back tears at her neighbours' misery, moved among the crowd organizing places for the wounded men and offering hurried words of comfort to bereaved families. Her most important work was yet to be done and she knew that it would be hours before she had properly attended to all the casualties. Later in private she could grieve for the shattered families and the friends who had died. She took little notice when Delroy thanked her for her efforts before leaving to organize the defence of the town.

He appropriated the sheriff's office and placed Duke with the mule in the small corral behind the building after putting fodder from the dead man's supply into the manger attached to the corral rails; there was water in a trough. He would attend to the animals properly after handling more urgent business.

Wilde and a couple more equally grim-faced citizens were in the office when he returned. There was an air of panic about them as they crowded around the lawman. At first they mumbled among themselves but finally Wilde asked, 'What happens now, Marshal?'

'How do we recover the bodies of our people?' another asked.

Then the floodgates seemed to open and men started firing questions at the lawman.

Delroy raised his hands in a calming gesture 'just steady up a minute, gents, and we'll figure out what needs to be done first.'

'What do you reckon?' an elderly resident demanded.

'As I see it, our most important job is to protect the town until we can get more help. Based on what was told me,

King Lesley could have as many as thirty men in his gang. It just depends upon how many are away robbing the countryside at the time.'

A look of horror came over the questioner's face. 'Oh Lord. We sent Henderson out with possibly half that number and were sure he had enough men. He wanted to wait but we pressured him to go. We got all those men killed.'

Another council member sought self-justification claiming. 'We provided him with a good scout that we hired specially. They should not have ridden into a trap like that. It's their own fault.'

'I don't care who was to blame,' Delroy interrupted. Under the circumstances they would gain little by apportioning blame. 'We need to get this town protected; I'll telegraph to my boss for a few more men.'

'You can't,' said Ross Fulton, the telegraph operator who was standing at the back of the room. 'Somebody's cut the wires. The town is isolated.'

4

Night fell on a very nervous town. The citizens, at Delroy's urging, had scraped together all available firearms and posted sentries at strategic points. Another group slept at the sheriff's office, ready to respond to any alarm.

Mort Wolfe stood on the balcony of the hotel, his rifle cradled in his arms and looking west toward the San Christobals. He was too nervous to be tired. King Lesley was somewhere out in the darkness. They had met before. Was it only two years ago?

He recalled the impact of the bullets and the scream of his wife as they were shot down. The outlaw had wanted their horses and supplies and the lives of a young couple on a struggling ranch meant nothing to him. Attracted by smoke from the burning ranch house, neighbours had found him barely alive, but all they could do for his beloved Maryanne was to bury her. After several painful months, Wolfe's wounds had healed and he had set out on his mission of vengeance but he was a different man. He was nervous and indecisive and at times of stress actually trembled. Much as he loathed Lesley there were times when his fear almost overcame his desire for revenge because he knew that alone there was little he could do. It seemed impossible that he could stop the bandit's depredations. But despite his misgivings, he drove himself and hoped that someday he might see the outlaw over gun-sights. Meanwhile his life was anxious and empty. A desire for revenge still smouldered within him but it seemed unlikely that it would ever be fulfilled. He was just about broke when he arrived at Henly Springs and had been forced to sell his horse and rifle just to live. It was too soon to count on a favourable change of fortune, but to a degree his situation had improved. He

41

had another rifle, courtesy of the outlaws, was being fed as one of the town's defenders, and best of all, had been able to hit back against Lesley's gang. Despite this, a nagging doubt suggested to him that he was on the losing side and that the bandit would triumph again.

At the other end of the town Rose Allen was nearing exhaustion. For hours she had been treating the wounded in a makeshift hospital that normally did duty as a meeting hall. Several women from the town were helping but she was the only one with sufficient expertise to properly tend the injuries. Wearily she sat in a chair and her heavy eyelids began to close. Just as sleep was about to claim her, someone called, 'Rose'. She was needed again.

After replacing a dressing that had come loose, the girl seated herself close to the most seriously wounded man who had finally drifted off to sleep. Almost immediately her eyes became heavy again.

Delroy found her there. 'Miss Allen,' he said quietly.

Rose awoke with a start.

'You have done all that you can here. Go home now and rest,' the marshal said.

'I'm needed here, Marshal.'

'You'll be needed more tomorrow. Let me take you home now. Folks here will know how to find you in an emergency. This town needs you, so by looking after yourself you are also serving them. Come on now, I'll walk you home.'

'There is no need for an escort, Marshal. It's not far.'

'You could be right, Miss Allen, but tonight is not like other nights. King Lesley could well try raiding the town. We can't afford to lose you.'

Rising to her feet, Rose arranged for another woman to watch the patients and left the building with Delroy holding her elbow. Her feet felt like lead.

There was not much conversation except that they were on a first name basis by the time the girl reached home.

43

* ★ ★

King Lesley watched the distant lights of the town being extinguished as people finally sought their beds. He took another swig from the whiskey bottle he held. The day had been a busy one for him. The ambush of Sheriff Henderson had been a great success but the loss of four men had taken some of the shine off it. Losing Ned Curtis had been unfortunate because of late he had been increasingly reliant upon him. He cared little for the other men but the skirmish had been a blow to his prestige. Strangers had ventured into his kingdom and killed some of his bandits. They needed to be taught a lesson.

Already he had isolated the town by cutting the telegraph wires. He had also placed ambushes on the two roads connecting Henly Springs with neighbouring towns. His men had been instructed to allow people in but to let nobody out. He had a reliable spy in town and would know when the townspeople moved against him. His keen-eyed lookouts were always posted in daylight hours and were alert for any danger signals. He knew where his men were at all times and could quickly reach them with mounted messengers. Already he was calling in scattered parties of his raiders.

Another swig from the bottle and the bandit was ready to take on the world. In his youth he had ridden with Quantrill, the notorious butcher of the Civil War. He had been present when the guerrillas had sacked the town of Lawrence in Kansas.

Soon Henly Springs would pay an even greater price for intruding upon his kingdom. He would teach them a lesson that they would never forget. Silently he vowed that he would make Lawrence look like a Sunday-school picnic.

5

Ross Fulton halted his buckboard in front of the sheriff's office. Delroy saw him through the front window and went out onto the boardwalk to investigate.

The telegraphist was a tall, stoop-shouldered man with drooping jowls that made him look like a woebegone bloodhound. His mood matched his appearance. 'Marshal,' he said, as he juggled the reins of a pair of fractious mules, 'I need an escort. I'm going out to find and fix the break in the telegraph line, but I don't fancy going out alone. I think that the coyotes that cut the wire might still be waiting around.'

'So do I,' the lawman agreed. 'The Apaches often used to cut the wire and set a trap for those who came to fix it. Lesley and his men are quite capable of the same trick. Give me a couple of minutes to saddle up and get a bit of help and I'll go with you.'

Saddling up was easy enough, but recruiting help was a little more difficult. Most were loath to leave the security of the town. Aware of what had happened to a well-armed posse, the citizens did not like the chances of small groups venturing into King Lesley's territory.

Wolfe saw the situation and slunk away before he was noticed. He was tempted to volunteer, but wanted to live long enough to see King Lesley over the sights of his gun. He doubted that the bandit chief would be involved in a small-scale ambush. There seemed little point in risking his life when there was only a minimal chance that his enemy would be on the scene.

Crowley was different. Red-eyed and hung over from another long night in the saloon, he was still prepared to take a ride outside the town. When Delroy asked him he did not hesitate and minutes later joined them as they travelled out on the Belle Ridge road. Only then did he regret his decision as his headache seemed to increase with every step that his horse took.

The marshal left Crowley with the buckboard while he scouted ahead. Thanks to the field-glasses he had taken with him, he could examine the telegraph wire that ran parallel to the road while still some distance away. There were plenty of prospective ambush sites along the road but he was gambling that any trap would be set at the break in the wire.

He left the road, steering Duke behind as much cover as possible and hoping that any watchers were concentrating on the trail. Then, thanks to the morning sun glinting on the wire, he saw the break. It was on an open flat about a quarter of a mile ahead. There would be little cover for anyone making repairs.

Delroy's next task was to locate where the ambushers would be lurking so he reasoned that they would not be far from the break in the line. On his side of the trail there was a clump of brush big enough to conceal a few horses. Deciding that was the most likely spot, he trained the glasses on it. In seconds he detected a light-coloured buckskin horse partially visible among the dark-green leaves. Then, through a break in the foliage, he caught a glimpse of brown, another horse. The clump was not big enough to conceal more than three horses so the lawman correctly assumed that the party was not a big one. Where were the men?

Something black moved into the lawman's line of vision — a hat. Lowering the glasses slightly, he saw the head and shoulders of a man in a blue and white checkered shirt and, more ominously, the barrel of a repeating rifle. As he watched, another man with a red beard showed himself and pointed up the trail where Crowley and Fulton had just moved into view. In another two minutes they would be in range of the hidden gunmen.

Delroy could plainly see the man with the beard as he raised his rifle. Slipping out of his saddle, he drew his carbine and sighted on the unsuspecting rifleman. He also dispensed with all legal niceties. The bandit was prepared to kill without warning and in Delroy's book he had not earned the option of surrender even in the unlikely event that he would consider such a course. Sighting quickly, he squeezed the trigger. As the butt plate pushed against his shoulder and he heard the thump of a bullet striking home, the lawman was seeking his next target. A bush moved violently so he fired into the centre of it. He caught a glimpse of a man in a grey coat whose presence he had not detected previously. He reeled away out of sight as a bullet knocked him sideways.

The unwounded member of the group guessed the direction of Delroy's attack, threw himself onto the buckskin horse and fled. He broke out onto the trail where the trees partially screened him from the lawman and plied his spurs viciously.

Delroy sent a few shots after him but decided against wasting further ammunition as the range increased.

Hoofs rang on the hard clay road as Crowley came charging into the fight, but the fugitive gunman had a long start on him. Jumping into Duke's saddle, Delroy rode to intercept his companion. 'Stop, Frank,' he called. 'Stop.'

Crowley sat his horse back on its haunches and slid to a halt as the lawman emerged from the brush before him. 'There are a couple in the brush there. I think they've been hit but we had best make sure.'

Crowley dismounted. Both drew their six-shooters. This would be fast, close-range work where a rifle would be a disadvantage. They left the horses standing, reins down, moved a few yards apart and entered the brush. A short distance ahead they could see the bearded man lying with the awkward sprawl of one who has died violently and suddenly.

Where was the other man?

Delroy signalled by putting a finger to his lips then pointing. The only possible hiding place was a log lying in a tangle of tall weeds. Not far away two tethered horses were snorting nervously.

The marshal took one more step and a man with a gun rose halfway from concealment, his face bearing a grimace of desperation as he sought a target. The grimace turned to an expression of horror as he saw himself looking into the muzzles of two guns.

Crowley fired and the heavy bullet hammered the man back to the ground. He fired again a split second later, but the second bullet struck a man already dead.

'Good shooting,' Delroy said, as he uncocked and holstered his gun. 'Now let's drag this pair out into the open where we can have a good look at them while Fulton tries to fix the wire.'

The cowhand chuckled. 'Fulton won't be fixing anything. As soon as he heard your shot, he turned those mules around and lit out. He won't stop this side of Henly Springs. Are we going after the one that got away?'

Delroy shook his head. 'We wouldn't catch him and might run into his friends. When we get this pair loaded onto their horses, I'll have a look and see if we can join up that wire again.'

The latter task proved impossible as the bandits had cut a long section of wire from the line and removed it. The marshal said nothing to Crowley but was secretly angry because he knew that Fulton had a portable Morse key among the tools in the buckboard. With that connected to the cut wire they might have been able to send a message.

A mile short of the town Delroy called a halt. He pointed to a ditch a short distance from the trail. 'We'll dump those bodies here after I write down a few details and collect their personal effects. Folks in town won't appreciate us bringing back a couple of dead bandits with their own men lying unburied out in that canyon.'

They worked quickly with an eye out for possible pursuers. As he wrote in his notebook, the marshal pretended not to notice the green dollar bills that Crowley had found in one dead man's pocket and quietly slipped into his own. He remembered how the cowhand had charged to his assistance and felt that he had earned the few dollars that the dead man could never use.

When the lawman had finished writing down the details and collecting a few personal items, they took the dead men's weapons and rolled the bodies into the ditch. After piling stones and logs on top they remounted and leading the captured horses, headed for Henly Springs.

The town was in uproar when they reached it. In his panic Fulton had imagined that the whole of Lesley's gang had attacked them. He sincerely believed that the others had both been killed.

Rose looked fresh and rested and smiled as the pair rode in. 'I'm glad to see that Mr Fulton was wrong,' she called from the doorway of the temporary hospital.

'So am I,' Delroy replied fervently.

6

Yaqui George spoke for his comrades when he asked their leader, 'When do we start hitting back?'

His mood not improved by his morning headache, Lesley snarled, 'When I say so. You sorry sonsabitches were nothing until I started thinking for you. Leave the planning to me.'

'The boys are getting restless,' Yaqui said apologetically. 'We never lost a man in a full year and now we've lost six in two days. They want to start hitting back.'

'They'll get their chance when those town coyotes come again. They are sure to. Their relatives are down there in the canyon getting eaten by wolves and buzzards and all sorts of things. People like that worry about their dead and they are sure to have a try at recovering the bodies. Next time we get them running, we'll follow them back to town and take the place apart. Once they start running they won't stop to fight.'

'But what if they manage to get more help from somewhere before they attack us again?' Yaqui persisted. 'They know now that getting in here is not going to be easy.'

His leader sneered. 'Half-a-dozen men with repeaters can hold that canyon all day. We have food and permanent water. They can't get in here.'

'But what if somehow they do?'

Ignoring his hangover, Lesley forced a laugh. 'Even if that happens we can get out through the desert behind us. Folks say there's no water there but I know a hidden spring that the Indians used. Tell the boys to trust their king, Yaqui. I know what I'm doing.'

* * *

Delroy visited the wounded men hoping to gain useful information about the disaster in the canyon. It puzzled him that an experienced scout like Harry Campbell had led the posse so deeply into the trap without noticing that something was amiss. He could only conclude that the elderly scout had lost some of his alertness as the years advanced.

Though he tried to convince himself otherwise, Delroy's visit was not all business. Rose Allen was there and he found himself enjoying her company immensely. She was warm and friendly to those in her care and spared no effort to make them more comfortable. With the marshal, she was relaxed and, despite the serious nature of her work, was ever ready to laugh when some lighter moment presented itself. He would happily have lingered at the hospital if it had not been for the responsibility that the towns-people had placed upon him. As the only lawman in Henly Springs, he found himself elected to lead the town's defence even though such tasks were normally carried out at county rather than federal level. This role forced him to ration the time that he spent in Rose's company.

A group of men was waiting in the street for him when he returned to the office. They were standing around a thin youth who held the reins of a lanky, thoroughbred horse. John Lindsay, as he introduced himself, had volunteered to ride his uncle's racehorse to Belle Ridge with news of the town's plight. The citizens were sure that a large posse would come to their aid. Delroy did not like the idea and said so.

'There's nothing can catch this horse,' the owner boasted.

'A bullet can catch him,' Delroy reminded.

The uncle, a small bow-legged man immediately argued, 'You and Crowley cleared away the bandits on the Belle Ridge road. It should be safe enough.'

The marshal disagreed. 'If King Lesley is only half as smart as I think he is, he'll have closed that avenue of escape very quickly. That break in the telegraph wire was not designed to be just a temporary inconvenience to us.'

He turned to the young man. 'John, I can't let you go. It's too dangerous.'

An angry chorus of disapproval came from the assembly.

'It ain't any of your kin, rotting out there in that canyon,' an angry voice shouted.

Delroy raised his hands and tried to placate the crowd and, while his attention was diverted, a few men moved between him and the horse. A second later the boy was in the saddle and spurring hard out of town.

'Stop!' the marshal called.

His order was ignored.

'What are you going to do now, Marshal — shoot him?'

Delroy looked angrily at the questioner. 'I won't need to. Someone else will most likely do that.'

As he looked after the galloping rider, the marshal again saw a puff of white smoke suddenly erupt from the restaurant chimney. It lasted only a second or two and the smoke turned grey again. He started to wonder. It was obvious that some new fuel had been added to the fire in the stove. Was it just a coincidence that it had happened twice when riders had left town?

The crowd dispersed and Delroy returned to the battered desk in what had been Sheriff Henderson's office. Unfinished correspondence had been crammed into the left-hand drawer. The right one contained keys, handcuffs and boxes of various types of ammunition.

Like a rock in his boot, that puff of white smoke was worrying him. He told himself that it was nothing, but the image lingered in his brain. Finally he decided to resolve the issue. There was the distinct possibility that he was suffering from an over-active imagination but he had to be sure. He rose, looked about and saw a large brown envelope. An old newspaper lay in the corner of the room. He took a page out of it, folded it carefully and placed it in the envelope. Now he needed someone reliable.

He guessed that Crowley would be in

the saloon but was unsure just how sober he would be. Then he remembered Wolfe. The drifter was smart enough but his nervous manner was a problem. There was a chance that he might refuse his request, but he was worth trying.

Wolfe was grooming a horse in Kopper's livery stable when Delroy found him. The proprietor was having an afternoon nap.

Delroy wasted no time in small talk. In a quiet voice he outlined his plan. A haunted look came into the drifter's eyes. For a couple of seconds, it seemed that he would refuse but then he swallowed hard and in a shaky voice, said, 'I'll do it.'

'That's good,' Delroy told him. 'Just come up to the office when you are ready to ride. I'll have Duke ready. Pick a time when there are plenty of people about; the more who see you, the better.'

Fed and well rested, the bay horse would catch any horse-lover's eye and his coat shone like satin when his owner brought him from the corral and hitched him to the rail in front of the office. A couple of bystanders were admiring him and others, sensing that something different was about to happen, lingered on the boardwalk.

Wolfe arrived with a saddle on his shoulder. He could have used the marshal's but Delroy had wanted him to be noticed. The bigger the show, the greater crowd it would attract.

Delroy came out of the office and proceeded to describe the horse's peculiarities as the drifter cinched his saddle into place. When he was ready to mount, the marshal produced the envelope. He passed it to Wolfe who stuffed it in a side pocket of his coat. 'Give this to the sheriff at Sullivan's Flat.'

'Are you sure the road's clear?' Wolfe asked nervously. He was not really acting.

'I reckon it is now,' the lawman replied. 'Lesley's men will all be going in the other direction after that young jackass on the racehorse.'

A grey-haired woman standing nearby said sternly, 'Marshal, I don't approve of you using that young boy for bait.'

Delroy had gotten to know some of the townspeople over the last few days and now said harshly, 'Mrs Sinclair, you might recall that I tried to stop that boy leaving because I thought he would surely be killed. You people sent him, not me.'

Moving over to where Wolfe had just mounted Duke, he said quietly, 'Don't go too far out of town because Lesley probably has that road staked out. Just get out of sight and hide for fifteen or twenty minutes.' Then in a louder voice, the lawman said, 'Time you were on your way, Mort.'

Wolfe turned the horse with a flick of the rein and the sunlight rippled on its powerful muscles. A slight squeeze of the legs and the horse jumped into a canter.

While the onlookers were watching

the horse, Delroy had his eyes fixed on the restaurant. The thin trickle of grey smoke became a puff of white. Seconds later it was gone. Delroy had seen enough.

Drawing his gun as he went, he sprinted across the street and, none too gently, threw open the restaurant door. Two ladies enjoying coffee together almost dropped their cups as the lawman ran around the end of the counter, ignored the startled waitress and charged into the kitchen.

A big man in a white apron was standing by the stove and the door to the firebox was open. Beside him was an open canister of sugar. He looked around in surprise.

'Get your hands up,' Delroy snapped. 'You're under arrest.'

For a second the man seemed speechless and shocked, but then he found his voice. 'Who the hell do you think you are, charging in here waving a gun? I haven't done anything wrong.'

'That's your story, but I think you

have been signalling King Lesley every time someone leaves this town. This is the third time I've seen a puff of white smoke from your chimney.'

'I don't know what you are talking about — I have not left my restaurant all day.'

'You don't have to. There was an old civil-war partisan trick. A handful of sugar thrown into a stove produces a puff of white smoke. It only stays a second or two but that's enough for those who might be watching for it. Now you don't appear to be cooking anything so what is that sugar doing beside you?'

Anger welled up in the big man and for a second he looked as though he would launch himself at the lawman. But he saw the bore of Delroy's gun muzzle aimed at him like an unblinking, black eye and quickly realized that a wrong move could well prove fatal. Instead he resorted to bluster. 'I don't know what you are talking about. No court is going to convict a cook for having a fire and sugar in a kitchen.'

Delroy gave a slight smile. 'Who said this matter is going to court? Those two lady customers of yours heard everything I just said and have bolted like a couple of scalded cats. I can just walk out of here and the people in this town will tear you to bits. You are responsible for a lot of grief around here. I reckon there's a lynch mob gathering already. If you talk I'll protect you; if you don't I'll turn you over to the mob. Nobody outside this town will ever know what happened. You don't have long.'

Stark fear showed on the man's face and his eyes darted about like trapped animals seeking to escape. In desperation, he lunged at the marshal. With the ease of long practice, Delroy's gun barrel slashed against the side of his head and the restaurant owner fell to his knees.

'I won't be so gentle if I have to do that again. I can hear a crowd coming. Now talk, or I walk away and leave you to the people whose menfolk you helped murder.'

Delroy's threat was a bluff but it was a convincing one.

'I'll talk,' the man whispered. 'Don't let them get me.'

7

Wolfe did not like to stray too far from town and turned about after a mile or so. Delroy had told him that he need not go far and he knew that Lesley's men were lurking somewhere along the road. He did not know what the marshal had been planning so had no idea whether his part in the charade had brought about the right result.

As he rode back into Henly Springs he saw a crowd gathered around the gaol. There was a buzz of conversation and the mood was angry. Spying Kopper on the edge of the gathering he rode across to him, leaned down from the saddle and asked, 'What's going on?'

'Delroy has arrested Wilf Grimmet — seems he was passing information to King Lesley when certain people left town. He was sending some sort of smoke signal from his chimney.'

Just then the door of the sheriff's office opened and the marshal came out onto the boardwalk.

'Why are you holding Grimmet?' a townsman called from the crowd.

'Is it right that he's in cahoots with Lesley?' another shouted.

Delroy raised his voice, as he replied, 'I have arrested Grimmet because I think he has been signalling Lesley. I don't need to tell you that we are in a bad spot here, but I will shoot anyone who tries to take this prisoner. It is important that we keep Grimmet alive because of the information he is prepared to give us. Also, he has not been convicted of any crime so forget any ideas of lynching him. It is in this town's interest that Grimmet remains alive. If you have trusted me this far, trust me now. I notice too that there are a couple of our sentries among you. I am not their boss, but I hope that you will persuade them to get back to where they should be. Lesley could attack this town any time he feels like it.'

The crowd turned their attention to a pair of men with rifles who turned away sheepishly and returned to their posts. The situation had been defused and the assembly was breaking into small groups, some walking away and others talking earnestly among themselves. Then the rattle of a wagon and pounding hoofs were heard from the other end of town.

Behind a six-mule hitch a wagon swung into the street. People scattered. Long before reaching the sheriff's office, the driver was jamming his foot on the brake and hauling back on the reins. His iron jawed team might have been harder to stop if they had not been forced to pull a heavy load at such speed. They were only too happy to halt although the wheel mules were forced to sit back in their breeching to slow the momentum of the load. The driver was nearly as wild-eyed as his team as he brought the wagon to a stop in a swirl of dust. 'Where's the sheriff?' he called.

'There's been a murder.'

Delroy ran across the street. 'I'm a US Marshal. What's the trouble?'

'Have a look over the tailboard, Marshal. I found this young feller shot full of holes. He was lying a few miles back on the Belle Ridge trail.'

The lawman knew who the victim would be even before he unfastened the tailboard chains. When he did, the corpse of John Lindsay stared back with sightless, wide-open eyes.

'Did you see any sign of who did this?' Delroy asked.

The driver had left the box and was standing beside him by then. 'I sure did. There was four of them. They came out of the brush just after I picked up the body — just sat on their horses about a hundred yards away and watched me. I thought I was a goner. Then one of them called out that he would kill me if I tried to come back along the same road. I got out of there real quick.'

The teamster introduced himself as

Henry Dunne. His wagon contained bales of hay and sacks of oats for Kopper's stables. Sometimes he carried general freight between Belle Ridge and Henly Springs, but usually his cargo was horse fodder. 'They can't grow much feed around here,' he explained.

The crowd was gathering again and the dead boy's uncle pushed through them. 'Oh no,' he groaned. 'What will I tell my sister?'

'That's your problem,' Delroy said coldly.

He thanked Dunne for bringing the body in and then retreated to his office.

Wolfe had attended to Duke and was waiting for him there. The lawman explained how he had used him to flush Lesley's spy from hiding. This brought a rare smile to the drifter's face. He said he was pleased to be hitting back at Lesley.

'I'm looking for a deputy,' Delroy said. 'Are you interested?'

For a moment Wolfe's grey eyes showed a hint of panic. He thought for a while. 'Why me?'

'Because you are reliable.'

'Frank Crowley's more the man you want. He's scared of nothing.'

'Frank is inclined to rush into things. You use your head.'

Wolfe shook his head. 'I'm not as reliable as you think. The thought of going near Lesley scares hell out of me. I hate the man. He ruined my life and I would dearly love to kill him, but my nerve is gone. I frighten easily and just when you need me, I might run out on you.'

'I don't think you will. It took a lot of guts to say what you just told me. Think it over and let me know later. I have to see Kopper now. Let me know what you decide.'

The stable operator was forking hay into a large corral that held the horses captured from Lesley's men. The animals were eating hungrily. They had seen plenty of work. A couple had ribs showing and all had poverty lines on their hindquarters.

Delroy pointed toward the horses. 'Looks like life is tough on the other side of the law.'

'It would be up there where they've been living,' Kopper said.

'I heard you knew a bit about that San Christobal area that Lesley claims as his kingdom. Could you tell me about it?'

'I sure can. I did a bit of prospecting there years ago. Never found anything though. Come into the barn and have a cup of coffee and I'll tell you what I know.'

They talked for the next half-hour. Kopper explained that the main canyon led into a maze of smaller canyons. Contradicting what others had told the marshal, he explained that there were other ways into the area. The main canyon was the only entry for horsemen but a man on foot could easily enter by climbing over some of the surrounding hills. There was also a back exit from Lesley's kingdom, but it was guarded by fifty miles of desert. Anyone leaving by that means would need to carry a big supply of water. Any attackers coming from that direction would have to cross the desert and fight their way up a narrow canyon. If they failed to win through they were faced with a waterless retreat over fifty miles. Attacking from the western desert side was not a serious option.

Delroy knew that Lesley's lookouts would be able to see any force that approached the main canyon and the outlaws would have plenty of time to prepare an effective defence. 'So the place has no serious weaknesses that we could attack?'

The older man scratched his bald head for a moment. Then he said, 'There is one weakness: you saw it out there in the corral.'

'The horses?'

'That's right. If Lesley has about thirty men, as most folks assume he has, he could have as many as forty horses there, maybe even more. In this country a horse needs about ten acres of grass to survive all year round. From what I know, there isn't four hundred acres of grass in there. Lesley has been holed up there for at least two years and I reckon his horses would have eaten the place out by now. Lesley's men must not have known what Henry was carrying in the wagon when they let him through. I reckon they would be needing all the horse feed they can get round about now.'

Delroy rose and jammed his hat firmly on his head. 'That's mighty interesting. You've been a big help, Mr Kopper. I'll see what I can figure out.'

★   ★   ★

Lesley made his way through the collection of makeshift shacks that his men had constructed. There had been no effort to lay out an orderly camp and the temporary shelters had been rigged wherever their builders had considered convenient. The leader lived in comparative luxury in a cave dug into the

77

side of a hill. He found Yaqui in the shade of a cottonwood tree plaiting a rawhide quirt. The big half-breed looked up casually, He was one of the few who did not fear their leader.

Lesley did not waste words. 'The lookouts are saying that they haven't heard from Grimmet today.'

Yaqui carefully twisted one rawhide strand under another before replying. 'That ain't unusual, King. I think we have them people too scared to come out. There's no point in sending signals if there's nothing happening.'

His boss was not convinced. 'I want you to slip into Henly Springs tonight and see what's happening. Can you do that?'

'Easy as pie. Them tenderfeet are trying to guard too big an area and there's gaps everywhere between their sentries. I had a look a few nights ago. They're careless too. The fright has worn off and now they are not really expecting anything to happen.'

'Can you make something happen

— something very nasty? I want them really scared.'

Yaqui was not given to honesty, but when he tapped the Bowie knife on his left hip and said that the task would be a pleasure, he was speaking the truth. He loved killing people.

8

Wolfe decided that he would take the deputy's job and Delroy wasted no time in installing him in the office. He wanted to see Rose Allen before she stopped her hospital work for the day. He was just in time, as the girl was leaving the hall when he arrived.

'I'm glad I caught you, Rose. Have you eaten yet?'

She gave a tired smile, for the day had been a long one for her. 'I haven't, but I'll have something when I get home.'

'Would you like to join me for a meal at the hotel? I'm afraid that Grimmet's restaurant is no longer operating. It's my treat.'

Rose was really too tired to be preparing a meal and washing up later so she agreed on condition that she paid for her own food. The determined tilt to her chin told the marshal that she could not be persuaded to change her mind. Together they walked along the lamp-lit boardwalk to the hotel.

'Tongues will wag when the town busybodies see us dining together,' the girl laughed.

'Let them — I am in better company than you are.'

★   ★   ★

Yaqui left his horse half a mile from town. Sound carried a long way on a still night and he knew that it was safer to approach on foot. He had replaced his boots with moccasins and moved silently from one patch of shadows to the next.

His first task was to locate a sentry and this proved easier than he had expected. A match flared as the man lit his pipe. He was standing at the end of a lane between two buildings and would have been hard to detect if he had not betrayed his own presence. The man was already bored because he did not really believe that Lesley's men would dare attack the town. He would stand for a while, then move restlessly around the area before returning to his position.

Silently, the big half-breed glided a little closer, It was a moonless night but the guard was ruining his night vision by occasionally looking back at the town lights showing through the far end on the alley. This one would be easy. Yaqui knew that the right opportunity would soon present itself.

A short while later the sentry stopped his pacing, leaned his shotgun against a paling fence and prepared to refill his pipe.

He was not even looking in the right direction when a powerful hand was clamped over his mouth and he felt the paralysing pain as a knife was driven into one of his kidneys. He could not resist as that same knife was withdrawn and slashed across his carotid artery releasing a spurt of arterial blood. His death was quick and silent.

Yaqui let his victim fall and expertly rifled his pockets. He found a watch and a few coins that went into the side pocket of his jacket. Then he wiped his bloodstained hands and knife on the dead man's clothes and slid quietly into the alley. He was well pleased with himself as he now had an unguarded escape route when his work in the town was done. He even allowed himself to imagine the consternation among the townspeople when they found a couple of bloody corpses. Then the sound of footsteps on the boardwalk and the low murmur of voices brought him back to the task at hand. Quickly he ran to the mouth of the alley.

Keeping in the shadows, he risked a quick glance along the street. A man and a woman were approaching and a lamp on the other side of the road caught the glint of metal on the man's chest. He was a lawman. Yaqui knew well how the loss of such a man in the middle of the town would shatter any morale that the citizens might have built up. He would use his knife because he knew from experience that most people were particularly horrified by cold steel. Two men butchered in the middle of town would really throw a scare into Henly Springs. The woman did not matter. He would kill her if the chance arose, but she would serve his purposes just as well if she ran screaming through the town. He would be long gone by the time any help arrived.

Delroy was enjoying the walk back to Rose's place but after years as a government scout and more recently a peace officer, he had developed an inbuilt caution. While outwardly relaxed, he was still reading the scenery about him. The dark mouth of the alley automatically attracted his attention as a potential danger spot. Even as he glanced at it, the light from the lamp across the street caught the gleam of the knife blade as the half-breed moved forward. Instinctively he pushed Rose aside and turned to meet the killer as he charged out of the darkness.

By sheer good luck he blocked the knife thrust with his left forearm inside that of the attacker and simultaneously smashed a hard right to the man's jaw.

Yaqui reeled away and Delroy went for his gun but the killer's reactions were as quick as his own. A foot lashed out, caught his hand as he drew his Colt, and sent the weapon spinning from his grasp. 'Run, Rose!' he called urgently as Yaqui charged in again.

He whipped off his hat and caught the next knife thrust with that but the keen blade sliced through the felt and did not become entangled. Again he drove his fist into the dark face of his opponent, but this time Yaqui was ready and it was only a glancing blow.

'Is that the best you can do?' the killer snarled.

The roar of the Colt. 45 took both men by surprise, but Yaqui received the biggest shock. The bullet took him in the stomach and smashed him back to a sitting position on the ground. In shock he dropped his knife, but that left his right hand free for his gun.

Rose thrust the smoking Colt into Delroy's hand. 'Quick, he's still got his gun.'

The marshal wasted no time because he could see that Yaqui was far from finished. The range was short and he fired quickly knowing that he would score a hit somewhere. His target was hammered flat on his back by the bullet's impact, but the gun in the half-breed's hand seemed to have a mind of its own and swung toward him again.

But the movement was slow and Delroy had time to aim. His next shot tore through Yaqui's heart and the gun finally fell from his grasp.

Delroy turned to Rose. She was pale and trembling, her eyes still wide at the horror she had witnessed. 'Are you all right?' he asked.

She gave a an uncertain smile and said, in a small shaky voice, 'I will be soon.'

'You saved my life.' He moved closer and put an arm around her. By now she was trembling violently. It seemed only natural to kiss her cheek and say, 'Thank you, Rose.'

She did not seem to notice the kiss or feel his arms around her. Her mind was still reliving the previous moments. 'I have never fired a gun in my life — I shot a man, Rod.'

'I'm mighty glad you did. That shot was a good one.'

She shuddered. 'I am not even sure that I aimed properly — I just picked up your gun, held it in both hands and pointed it.'

'That's why these Colt .45s are so popular. They point naturally when you hold them. Will you be OK if I let you go? I can see some folks coming and I would like to see if I know our late lamented friend.'

A couple of men came running up and one of them was Frank Crowley. 'What's been happening? What was all the shooting?'

'Have a look in that alley, Frank. Someone tried to kill me and if it hadn't been for Miss Allen, he would have succeeded.'

A woman stepped forward. She had been one of Rose's assistants at the makeshift hospital. 'Come with me, Rose,' she said gently. 'You don't need to be here.'

Like someone in a trance the girl allowed herself to be led away.

A couple of men dragged the corpse out of the alley. One whistled in surprise. 'Hell — that's Yaqui George. I was robbed by him once. He's one of the meanest skunks in King Lesley's outfit. Lesley won't be too pleased when he hears about this.'

Much to Delroy's surprise, he found two watches when he searched the dead man. One was bloodstained and when the marshal opened the case he found a name engraved inside. Holding it up to the light, he asked, 'Does anyone know a Robert Massinger?'

'Sure,' a bystander said. 'We all know

Bob Massinger; he does carpentry jobs around here. He's been helping guard this place.'

The marshal snapped shut the watch case. 'I think his luck ran out tonight. Does anyone know where he was guarding?'

The realization hit home. One thin-faced man stepped forward with a worried look. He pointed. 'Bob relieved me tonight. We were guarding the back of the town from the end of this alley.'

'Let's have a look,' Delroy said in a voice that suddenly sounded tired. 'I'll be mighty surprised if he's still alive.'

9

Delroy and the town council agreed on one thing; the perimeter of Henly Springs was too big for them to guard safely. They needed more men. King Lesley's small but highly mobile force had effectively thrown a cordon around them. A few desperate people had tried to leave but had been driven back by gunfire.

Various strategies were put forward but every one was flawed in some way. There was no escaping the fact that there were insufficient men to effectively defend the town. Yaqui George had shown the weakness of their own chain of guards.

The mention of the dead outlaw caused another debate; what to do with his body. Most were in favour of dumping it out in the desert so that scavengers might devour it as they had their relatives and friends in the canyon. Delroy did not agree.

'If we dump Yaqui's body out in the desert, Lesley will know that he is dead. It's best if we keep him guessing. I say we should bury him somewhere around here. We have his horse so, as far as his boss knows, he could have deserted, been captured, or even changed sides. We should be trying to worry Lesley.'

'We need to do a damn sight more than worry him,' a townsman reminded him. 'We need to clear the roads so we can get help.'

Nathan Wilde, the storekeeper, interrupted him. 'Just hold your horses, Matt. Who is going to protect the town if our fighting men are out trying to clear the roads?'

'That's right,' another agreed. 'King Lesley could come down out of the mountains and take this place over in a few minutes.'

Wilde had discussed the problem earlier that day when Delroy had been buying a new hat at the store. 'I think the marshal might have a few ideas.' He pointed to the lawman. 'What do you think we should do?'

'I have a few ideas, but no immediate answer to our problem,' Delroy replied. 'Give me a day or two to get a bit more information. Meanwhile Miss Allen has come up with a very good idea. She has suggested that women can be used in places where they can see from second-storey rooms that face in the right direction. They are up out of danger but can see around the place. She is organizing that today.'

'Dang busybodies,' growled the man called Matt. 'They should be good at that. My mother-in-law spends half her life stickybeaking from our upstairs windows.'

'She sounds like a promising recruit,' Wilde laughed. 'Make sure that Rose knows about her.'

When the meeting broke up, Delroy made his way to the livery stable but paused on the way at the corral where the captured horses were kept. Taking a notebook and pencil he walked across to the bay horse that Yaqui had left tethered. He sketched the brand because he suspected that the animal had probably been stolen. A couple of ribs were visible under its dusty hide and grey sweat had dried in the poverty lines that showed on the animal's haunches. As he looked at it he had a vague feeling that horses might be important to his plans, but at present failed to see how they could significantly alter the situation.

Kopper was having an afternoon siesta but did not mind being woken up. As he clattered about his small kitchen preparing a pot of coffee, he asked the lawman the reason for his visit.

Delroy said, 'I want to know more about that canyon where Lesley hides out. Could you draw me a rough map. It need not be exact.'

Kopper thought for a while. Finally he said, 'I reckon I could. It's been nearly thirty years since I last prospected there but I can give you a rough idea.'

He took some sheets of writing paper from a desk in his tiny office and, pencil in hand, set out to draw a map. He ruined two sheets before he was satisfied with his sketch. With a gnarled finger, he indicated the places he considered important. 'This is the main canyon where our men got ambushed,' he said. 'It runs back about two miles and has a couple of twists in it. About a mile and a half in, another canyon leads off to the left. It runs about another mile. There's permanent water there and grazing for horses. I reckon that's where Lesley would have his camp. He certainly won't be down in the main canyon with all those dead men and horses.'

'Is there another entrance other than through the main canyon?'

Kopper's linger stabbed at a place to the left of the canyon entrance. 'Somewhere around here there was an old landslide. A horse can't get up it, But a man can. I reckon it would still be there. Chances are there're most likely a few other places too. The hills are not all that steep in some places for a man on foot. Lesley knows that no posse is likely to come after him without horses.'

'What do you know about a back exit to those mountains? A few folks have told me that there is one.'

'That's no secret but there's fifty miles of desert to cross if you try that way. I heard a story that there is an old Indian well halfway across if you know where to find it, but it's one hell of a risk. If you couldn't find it, or if it was dry, that would be the end of you. As long as King Lesley watches the main canyon, he won't need to guard his back. The desert does that.'

Delroy thanked the old man, carefully folded the map and, after putting it in his pocket, he left. An idea was starting to form in his mind. As yet he had not worked out the detail and would need more information before he could develop a proper plan.

He returned to the gaol and tried to

question Grimmet but the latter would only protest his innocence. He stuck to his story that he had no connection with Lesley and it was obvious that he would not co-operate.

Next the lawman outlined his plan to Wolfe. The new deputy did not like it and said so. But Delroy reassured him by saying that he would not be involved. 'I need someone here to take care of things in case I don't make it back. That's your job. I'll get Frank Crowley to help out with what I am planning to do.'

'Crowley is crazy enough to go along with it, but be careful. There are times when he is likely to charge in without thinking.'

'That's why I want you here, Mort. You use your head.'

★ ★ ★

King Lesley watched the new riders coming into camp and smiled in satisfaction. There were five of them and he was hoping that others would soon join them. He had sent messengers around various outlaw networks. The newcomers had worked with him before and had demonstrated a suitable lack of regard for the well-being of the general population. Now, attracted by the promise of plunder, they were joining forces with him again. He was relieved to see Murray Halloran riding at the head of the group. With Curtis dead and Yaqui away, he needed a good right-hand man and Halloran would fit the bill.

His new ally was a short, heavily built man with a battered face that showed a certain familiarity with barroom brawls. But he was smarter than many criminals and utterly ruthless.

Yaqui's absence nagged at him though, as did the silence from Grimmet, but in the latter's case, he suspected that nobody dared venture from town. There was little point in alerting sentries if the townspeople were staying close to home.

Yaqui seemed to have disappeared off the face of the earth and his leader suspected that he had been killed or captured, but had no way of knowing. Grimmet would signal when he had information to sell but so far there had been nothing.

Halloran rode over to Lesley's side and introduced his men by first names or nick-names only. They were eager for loot. Leaning on his saddle horn he said, 'From the message you sent, it sounds like you have something big on the way, King.'

'I sure have. Come back here when you let your horses go. I'll get someone to show you where to put them and where to set up camp. Then we can have a drink. You probably have a lot of dust to wash out of your throat.'

'Sure have,' Halloran agreed. 'We covered better than thirty miles today. You know, King, I'm getting too old for all this travelling. I wish I could find a safe hideout like you have here. Being chased all over the country gets mighty tiresome. What is the story about you and the Henly Springs posse? From what I saw on the way in, you chewed them up pretty bad. They sure don't make the main canyon smell any sweeter. Can't you get rid of those bodies?'

An evil smile came to the outlaw leader's face. 'It suits me to leave those bodies where they are. It must annoy hell out of the folks in Henly Springs. It's only a matter of time before some hot-head has another try at collecting his dead relatives. They'll try again and lose men that they can't afford to lose. Sooner or later they'll take the bait. Then I'll really take that town apart.'

Halloran thought for a while, pushed back his hat and passed his shirtsleeve over his sweaty forehead. 'I ain't sure those town folks are all that dumb,' he said at length.

'Never underestimate the power of sentiment,' Lesley chuckled. 'When hearts start ruling heads, folks do crazy things. It's only a matter of time before their indignation overrules their fear. Then it will be time to teach them another lesson.' He indicated a heavily armed man who was approaching. 'Here is Herb. He'll show you where to drop your stuff and where to let your horses go.'

'We'll put our horses away and come back to join you in that drink,' Halloran promised.

10

Delroy made his preparations with care, He replaced his Cuban-heel riding boots with a well-worn pair that had low heels, and filled a couple of large water canteens. In the roomy pockets of a warm coat he placed paper-wrapped parcels of biscuits and jerked beef. The desert night would be cold enough and he saw no reason to add to his discomfort by being hungry as well. Though not particularly thirsty, he drank deeply from a bucket of well water he had drawn earlier. The more water in his system, the better he would be able to withstand the effects of the desert heat.

Wolfe looked at him and shook his head. 'I still reckon you're loco. You'll last about as long as a jack-rabbit at a coyote convention if Lesley's men pick up your tracks.'

'If I didn't think I could pull this off, I wouldn't be trying, Mort. If ever we hope to break Lesley's grip on this town, we have to find out his weaknesses.'

Any further discussion was cut short by the sound of a rider at the back of the building. Crowley had arrived. Slipping into his coat, the lawman picked up his carbine, the two canteens and his field-glasses.

'Good luck,' Wolfe said, as Delroy hurried out the door.

A few whispered words to the cowhand while he secured the extra equipment to his saddle, then he mounted and the pair rode out of town. Avoiding the trail they rode in a westerly direction. Ahead the San Christobal mountains loomed black against the star-studded sky. The only landmark was a notch in the mountain range so the pair rode straight at it. The arid ground was rough and supported many clumps of mesquite and cactus but they held their horses down to a

102

steady walk, trusting that the animals' better night vision would keep them out of trouble.

Both knew that sound would carry far in the night stillness so there was no conversation. There was little they could do about the unavoidable sounds of shod hoofs striking rock, or the creaking of leather. Occasionally a horseshoe struck a spark from a rock and the pair could only hope that the outlaws had no scouts hiding in the gloom. Delroy was gambling that Lesley felt safe from any night attacks and would put his sentries out only in daylight. The thought of the frightened citizens of Henly Springs making a night attack against his fortress seemed ludicrous.

Two hours' riding brought them close under the walls of Lesley's kingdom. They knew they were close to the main canyon as the smell of death hung in the air. The horses snuffled nervously.

'I'll leave you here,' Delroy whispered. 'Can you find your way back here around this time tomorrow night?'

Crowley looked up, noted the outline of the horizon against the sky and said confidently, 'I can find this place again. Just make sure you are here. I don't like hanging around this place.'

'That makes two of us,' Delroy said softly, as he hung the canteens from his shoulders and the field-glasses from his neck. Heavily laden he moved into the shadows cast by the rocky walls above. Crowley rode away leaving him feeling alone and exposed but there was no turning back.

After half an hour groping and stumbling in the dark he found sloping ground that told him he was at the old landslide. Twisting his carbine into the canteen straps to free his hands, he started up the slope. It was hard work hauling himself up by handholds on projecting rocks or bushes that grew in places where there was a bit of soil. Occasionally he would halt and listen while recovering his breath, but he heard no suspicious sounds from above.

Almost at the top of his climb he found a rocky overhang screened by a few stunted bushes. He knew that it would be safe from observation from above although it might be visible to someone on the plain below. But that was a chance he had to take.

Unslinging the equipment he had around him, he had a big drink of water and ate a little food. Then he buttoned his coat around him and settled down for what he knew would be a short but uncomfortable night.

The rock beneath him was hard and uneven and the coat only protected his upper body. The cold desert night chilled his legs and feet preventing sound sleep though he did manage short periods of rest. It was almost with relief that he saw the first signs of dawn appearing although the day ahead promised little but danger.

Taking stock of his position, Delroy saw no need to change the location. Overhanging rock concealed it from above and though observers further along the rim rock could see it from either side, a few bushes growing nearby offered a reasonable degree of concealment. By mid morning, the area would be in shadow which added to its chance of remaining undetected.

He ate what remained of his food and drank the last of the water in the first canteen. Shrugging out of his coat, he left that with the full canteen. The lawman knew that he would need the field-glasses but wondered for a while about his rifle. His main aim was to remain undetected and if things went wrong to the extent that he had to resort to his guns, he would have little chance. Finally reasoning that he needed to damage the bandits as much as possible before they killed him, he picked up the Winchester. It would hold attackers at a distance for longer and do more damage than his six-gun.

The morning sun was already warming the rocks and Delroy needed to watch where he was walking and putting his hands because it was a bad time for snakes. They would be coiled on the rocks absorbing the morning heat. One big rattler reluctantly moved out of his way just as he reached the top of the rim rock.

He peered over the edge but saw only boulders, twisted juniper trees and the odd clump of cactus. Remaining concealed, he looked about him but could see no sign of sentries looking over the plain below. It seemed that King Lesley knew that any posse would not leave Henly Springs before daylight and so there was no need to post lookouts too early.

Delroy resisted the urge to hurry and moved carefully from one patch of concealment to another. He was glad that he did so because at one point the heard a murmur of voices and two men emerged from the brush just as he threw himself into a clump of tall weeds. They were about fifty yards from him but never looked in his direction as they passed. He assumed that they were sentries going to their post overlooking the town, probably watching for Grimmet's signals.

Half a mile ahead, the lawman saw smoke rising from what was obviously a canyon and knew that he had found Lesley's camp. From that point he remained under cover until he had scrutinized his surroundings thoroughly. Experience as an Indian scout had taught him that early in the morning people became busy in the vicinity of camps and an unexpected confrontation would be disastrous.

Finally he reached a place where he could see down into a long, narrow canyon. His position was near the back of it above a trampled dust bowl that held a number of horses. Back toward the canyon's mouth his binoculars revealed a rough temporary fence with a strange collection of shelters and little groups of men around cooking fires.

At one stage he had entertained the vague idea that it might be possible to stampede the outlaws' horses but now saw that such an idea was impossible.

Directly below him he saw a small mustang-type chewing at the mane of another horse and remembered what Kopper had said about the lack of feed in the canyons. The classic signs were there: a knot of hungry horses clustered around the gate hoping that their masters would bring them a little to eat. Others that should have been grazing, stood with drooping heads. As usual the larger animals had lost the most condition because they required more fodder to keep going. Even the smaller ones though, were starting to look scrawny and dispirited.

The lawman counted fifty-three horses and of these, there were scarcely a dozen that were fit enough for hard work. He figured that these were later arrivals. It was time to move closer.

Taking advantage of every piece of cover, Delroy worked his way along the top of the canyon until stopped by a broad patch of bare rock where he could be seen if he tried to cross it. Reluctantly he decided that he could get no closer. Peering from under a bush he studied the men in the camp below.

They were the usual mixture; mostly Americans but with a few half-breeds and Mexicans. Most were heavily armed although they were in a safe camp. Some looked young enough to be teenagers and only a few were approaching middle age. Outlaws rarely grew old.

A cave faced Delroy's position and it seemed to be attracting more traffic than any other shelter. Men were coming and going and once he saw a plate of food being taken into it.

Then a group of men emerged. In their midst strode a small, scruffy, bearded man and the morning sun glinted on the nickel plating and mother-of-pearl butts of the twin revolvers he wore.

Delroy knew that he was looking at King Lesley.

11

'We need to do something about feeding those horses,' Halloran growled. 'Some of them are so poor that they have to stand in the one place twice to make a shadow. You have a problem here, King.'

'Horses are a dime a dozen. We can always steal more,' Lesley told him dismissively.

The other outlaw was not convinced. 'Well, you had better start stealing them pretty damn quick. Half those horses you have would be too weak to do a day's work.'

'You worry too much, Murray. They're only horses. There's plenty around here. This lot will do to get us to Henly Springs.'

Halloran frowned. 'You've been too long up here in this safe little hidey-hole,' he said. 'If ever you need to run from the law, you are going to need something better under you than the crow bait you have here. I'm telling you, King, you have a lot of men, but you can't use half of them because their horses are starved.'

'I suppose you have some suggestions?'

'I sure do. A couple of miles north of here we came through a big, grassy flat. We should drive the horses out there and shepherd them around for a couple of days until they get a good feed into them. Then we hit Henly Springs. Once there we can help ourselves to new horses and even a bit of feed for the best of these. We can't take all the horses out at once. We need to keep a few here but things can't go on like they are.'

Lesley was not one to bother with minor details and already he was feeling like a drink. 'Fix it your way, Murray. I don't care if horses are fat or lean as long as they do the job.'

Halloran departed shaking his head

and wondering if teaming up with Lesley was such a good move. Since their last meeting the latter's increasing dependence upon whiskey had become noticeable.

Across the canyon, Delroy was trying to count the men in the camp. Aware that some could be away and that he might not be able to see others, he estimated that Lesley had at least thirty men in his private army. Henly Springs people could not raise as many fighting men, nor could they match the bandits for weaponry. Outside help would be needed.

As he watched, the marshal saw a group of men saddling their horses. When all were mounted two waited at the lowered rails of the horse pasture while the others rode in and gathered the horses together. Then when the small herd was walking toward them, the pair at the gateway moved off and the loose animals followed them. Being half starved the horses had little energy and were prepared to follow the riders in front and move quietly ahead of those who herded them from behind. Two of the riders remained in the camp, but the other four helped drive the horses down to the main canyon.

From his eyrie high in the rocks Delroy silently bemoaned the lost opportunity. Separating Lesley's men from their horses would greatly restrict their ability to raid the town and the trails around it.

The sun was hot and he was thirsty so the marshal carefully retreated, moving back over the hill to where he had spent the night. Aware that two sentries were somewhere ahead of him he crept carefully, only crossing open ground after examining the surroundings first from cover. He was so intent on the danger ahead that he was not expecting any from where he had just been.

A cheery whistle came from a short distance behind him and he dropped instantly to the ground counting on a few low bushes and his immobility to conceal him. Peering from under the weeds, he saw a man come around a rock barely thirty yards away. He was tall and strolled carelessly along, his rifle held over his shoulder by the barrel. Suspecting nothing and whistling cheerfully, the bandit did not even glance in the marshal's direction.

Delroy scarcely dared to breathe until the man disappeared into the brush. Now there were three men ahead of him. He found a spot screened by a large clump of cactus and settled down to watch and listen. He was hot and dry and eager to get back to his hideout, but knew that it was safer to wait.

His caution paid off because a few minutes later the first pair of sentries walked past him on their way back to camp. For some reason they had been replaced by a single man. Aware that the other sentries had positioned themselves well away from his hideout, the lawman moved more confidently even if as quietly as he could.

He had reached the edge of the brush

and was at the rim rock above the landslide. A dust cloud away to the north showed the progress of the outlaw horses. While watching this, he found, in the worst possible way, where the new sentry had positioned himself.

A startled oath came from almost ground level and a man lying in the shade of a bush bounded to his feet. As he straightened, he brought up the Henry rifle he had been holding.

Delroy swung his rifle barrel and caught the man on the side of the head. He staggered but did not go down. His right hand was already working the Henry's lever, jacking a cartridge into the breech. A shot would bring the other outlaws running. With his left hand, he grabbed the Henry's brass receiver and managed to get his thumb in front of the hammer, preventing its fall. This time he tried to smash the steel-shod butt of his carbine into the other man's face but the latter blocked the swing with his forearm. Smashing a heel as hard as he could on the sentry's instep forced the man off-balance and, as he reeled, his foot slipped and he fell to one knee. This time the lawman was able to connect with a stunning blow of his rifle butt. His opponent lost hold of the Henry and toppled backwards over the rim rock. His body raised dust as it hit the landslide twenty feet below, slid a few feet and lay still, either dead or unconscious.

Delroy moved quickly, placing the fallen rifle in his hideout and climbing down to where his late adversary was sprawled. The man was dead, his skull fractured in the fall. The lawman dragged the body under a rocky overhang and camouflaged it as best he could with bushes and small rocks. Only when this was done did he retreat to his shelter and started taking small sips from his canteen. Then, when his thirst was satisfied, he settled down and slept.

It seemed he had scarcely closed his eyes when a loud, angry voice awakened him. It came from the cliff top above.

'Link — where the hell are you?'

The western sun was throwing the shadows out onto the plain and Delroy could see that of a man moving around. It was a very long shadow and he realized that he had slept until late afternoon.

The man doing the shouting was obviously the dead sentry's replacement. After a few minutes of tramping around and bellowing, the noisy one left the scene.

Delroy knew that the man would be back, probably with a search party, and wondered if he should not move down to the plain and seek shelter there but eventually decided that he might be safer where he was. There was the chance that he could be caught in full view on the landslide or be sighted from above on the plain. Darkness was falling and he knew that a search party would have little chance of finding their missing man once the light failed.

Dusk was just changing to darkness when he heard voices again. There were several men and none sounded too keen on their task.

'I don't like this,' one voice complained. 'It's too easy to walk off the edge in this light.'

'I know that,' another said, 'but King says we have to have a good look around. When something happens to a sentry he wants to know why.'

A third man joined in. 'Let's sit here for a while and have a smoke. Then we go back and tell King that it's just too dark and we can start first thing in the morning. A lot of the rock around here is crumbling and Link probably stood in the wrong place and finished up on the plain below. I ain't in any hurry to join him.'

All agreed that further searching was pointless. For half an hour, Delroy heard them arguing and speculating upon Link's fate, then they left. Impatiently he waited for the hours to pass. The sooner he was away from Lesley's kingdom, the happier he would be. He tried to imagine where Crowley was with the horses and then the doubts started to creep in. The idea that the cowhand might linger too long at the saloon did little for his peace of mind. He wondered too where the outlaws had taken their horses. If Crowley arrived on time, they might try to find them. Without their horses Lesley's men were nowhere near as dangerous.

12

Delroy guessed it was time to go, swallowed the contents of the last canteen and prepared to descend the cliff. The empty canteens would only be a noisy encumbrance so he abandoned them together with the dead sentry's Henry rifle. Though it might have been a useful addition to the town's defences, the rifle could be more trouble than it was worth and he had no intention of swapping it for his own. His new Winchester with its .44.40 centre fire cartridge was superior in both range and hitting power and that would be difficult enough to carry. To keep both hands free, he removed the strap from one of the canteens and improvised a sling. Then, with rifle and binoculars slung about him and carefully feeling his way, he started the descent.

Every handhold and every foothold had to be tested before he placed his full weight on it for some of the rock was loose and there were places where sheer drops had to be avoided. Several times he dislodged stones and they fell a long way before he heard them striking the ground. Progress was slow but Delroy was taking no chances. Even a twisted ankle had the potential to be fatal in Lesley's kingdom.

Though the night was cold, he was perspiring freely by the time he was safely at the foot of the cliffs. First he studied the outlines of the rim rock above him until he was near the spot where Crowley had left him. Then he settled down to wait. The time dragged and the lawman was tempted to start walking but he knew that he might miss the cowhand in the dark.

Finally he heard a horseshoe clink against a rock and a short time later a horse snorted. An indistinct shape loomed up in the gloom and a saddle creaked. 'Frank, is that you?' he called, softly.

'Don't shoot, Marshal. It's me. How did things go?'

Delroy took his horse's reins and mounted before replying, 'I'll tell you when we get away from here a bit. Sound carries on these still nights. Lesley might have a few guards out.'

After covering a safe distance, the marshal related his experiences and questioned Crowley about events in town. The latter assured him that all was well there. He said that Wolfe had worked tirelessly organizing defences, even if some of the citizens resented being ordered about by someone they had considered to be a no-account drifter.

'Lesley has sent most of his horses out of the canyons in search of feed,' Delroy said. 'You know this area better than I do. Where do you think he would send them?'

'There are big grassy flats up along Parry's Creek. The closest good grazing would be there. That's probably where he sent them.'

'Good. Can you find it in the dark? There'll never be a better chance to cripple Lesley's operations.'

'Are you sure you ain't biting off more than you can chew, Marshal? How many men are with them?'

'There might be half a dozen but most will be asleep. They'll night herd those horses in shifts. An old cowhand like you would not have any difficulty driving about forty head of horses. You would have done a lot of that on ranches.'

'Sure I did,' Crowley admitted, 'but I didn't have outlaws shooting at me.'

'I'll handle the guards. You get those horses running. Aim them for Henly Springs if you can, but whatever you do run them as far as you can from Lesley's hideout. Without horses, he can't do much. This can really scuttle any plans he's making. Will you help?'

'Normally I ain't a public-spirited type but you've caught me at a weak moment. I'll go along just to see what happens.'

They rode for an hour and a half before passing through a belt of timber and emerging on a large plain. Half a mile to their left they glimpsed the red coals of a camp-fire that had burned low.

Delroy pointed toward the fire. 'That's where most of the men will be. Now we have to find the horses.'

They rode a little closer. A slight breeze was blowing in their faces. Knowing that horses always fed ahead of the wind, they knew that the animals would not be far away. Delroy and Crowley were in luck because they probably would not need to pass the camp to find the horses, but there was still the matter of the night guards. How many would there be?

'When we find those horses, get behind them and get them running,' the marshal said quietly. 'I'll handle the guards. No matter what happens to me, keep those horses running.'

'If what you're telling me about them being half-starved, there might not be much running in them.'

'I know that, but run them as hard as you can. That way, even if you are forced to leave them later, they won't be of much use to Lesley and his crew. When horses are in such low condition, it takes more than one good feed to build up their strength again.'

A short while later they heard horses moving about and the sound of the animals chewing off clumps of grass carried plainly through the night, Then they started seeing a loose collection of vague shapes grazing about contentedly.

A match flared suddenly about fifty yards ahead as the night herder lit a cigarette. Then they saw the red tip glowing as the man rode straight toward them. He was going to the front of the herd to stop the animals straying too far from camp as they fed. Soon he would detect the intruders.

'We can't guard prisoners; I'll have to shoot him,' Delroy whispered. 'You get around behind those horses and set them running. I'll keep between you and the others. Remember — don't wait for me.'

The night herder might have heard the voice because he suddenly checked his mount. 'Who's that?' he demanded.

A touch of the spurs and Duke bounded forward covering the intervening space before the guard fully realized what was happening. Crowley was about a horse length behind.

Sparks flew as the outlaw threw away his cigarette and went for his gun. He was too late.

Delroy fired three shots as quickly as he could cock and shoot and saw the man topple from his mount as it jumped away in fright.

Screeching like a Comanche, Crowley raced his horse toward the camp sending the panicked horses in the other direction. When he was sure that the last one was past him, he turned and followed the cloud of pale dust that showed in the stampede's wake. For good measure, he fired a couple of shots in the air.

Delroy rapidly punched the empty shells from his gun and had just snapped shut the loading gate on the refilled cylinder when he heard a rider approaching from the camp. He turned Duke and cantered away. The more ground his opponent's horse had to cover, the safer he would be. He wanted his pursuer far from help before turning on him. The man was riding hard — too hard when the weakened state of his mount, the darkness and the rough ground were considered. Delroy heard a cry of alarm and the sound of a horse falling. He saw the cloud of dust it raised as the animal crashed down. Thankful that another shooting was not necessary, he turned his mount and set off after the runaways.

They left an easy trail to follow. The dust still hung in the air and the pounding hoofs drummed loudly on the hard ground. Occasionally the marshal heard Crowley's voice in the distance as he urged on the herd.

Leaving the horses to Crowley,

Delroy remained behind and, as they neared the canyon mouth that was the entrance to Lesley's kingdom, he rode a little closer to the base of the cliffs ready to intercept any riders who should come from the main camp. It was well that he did for the lawman suddenly heard horses clattering over the rocky ground at the canyon's mouth. Riders were coming from the outlaw stronghold to investigate. More ominously he could hear Crowley yelling and urging on the horses he was driving. The first mad gallop had used up much of the strength that the animals had left and now they were slowing considerably.

Despite their weakened mounts, Delroy knew that Lesley's men would make a great effort to recapture their horses, even if they had to ride a few to death to do so.

He had to buy Crowley more time. Easing his Colt from its holster, the marshal turned his horse and rode back to intercept the pursuers.

13

Three riders loomed up out of the darkness, all riding hard and concentrating upon the sound of the horse herd. It is doubtful if they noticed Delroy as he sat his horse behind a clump of tall cactus. They were in easy range when he fired at the leading rider.

The Colt's report and the red muzzle flash caused the man's horse to shy violently into the path of the one coming behind. The foremost rider toppled from his saddle while the man behind frantically tried to avoid colliding with the loose horse. The third rider drew and fired at their attacker but the combination of the fast draw, poor light and moving horse reduced his shot to a token effort.

Delroy fired again and heard a startled yell from his target. He did not know whether he had scored a hit or only frightened the man but the bandit wheeled his horse away. By this time, the second outlaw had regained control of his horse, wheeled it about and charged.

A flick of the rein and the touch of a spurless heel had Duke spinning away to the left just as the outlaw opened fire. His shot missed. Delroy's return shot hit its mark. Doubled over and clutching his saddle horn the wounded man let his galloping horse carry him out of range.

The lawman did not pursue. Whether alive or dead, the fight had gone out of his opponents. Another light touch of the rein against his neck and Duke pivoted on his hindquarters and set off after Crowley and the loose horses.

Unlike fresh horses, the captured animals were reluctant to move at faster paces and Crowley was forced to drive some of the weaker ones with the end of his lariat. Dawn was breaking when they came in sight of the town.

Delroy caught up with Crowley and

his charges, then took over the herding while the cowhand rode ahead to warn the town's sentries. They did not want some trigger-happy guard firing into the dust cloud that he had mistaken for a mounted group of bandits.

Only the guards and a couple of early risers saw the slow procession of weakened, head-drooping horses shuffling down the street to the big corral beside the livery stable. As Delroy was closing the gate behind them, Kopper emerged from his barn. He looked at the new arrivals and growled, 'You've brought me a lot more hungry mouths to feed, Marshal.'

'I have, but some of them could be horses taken from Sheriff Henderson's posse and their legal owners can take them home as long as they can keep them somewhere safe. King Lesley is sure to come after more horses, because last night we really crippled his operations. He would be lucky to have a dozen horses left and the ones he has are as poor as crows.'

Kopper shrugged. 'I'd best get feeding these. I've lost my assistant now since you made Mort Wolfe a deputy. He's been giving orders like he was Napoleon or someone.' As an afterthought he added, as he eyed the new horses, 'My feed supplies won't last long at this rate.'

'I'm hoping this situation won't last too long because this will force a showdown with King Lesley.'

★　★　★

The bandit leader had finished half a bottle of whiskey by the time his men had fully appraised him of the night's débâcle. Some of his crew had been killed and a couple wounded. The latter would receive little sympathy from their leader to whom they would only be a further encumbrance. When he called in the men guarding the breaks in the telegraph line he reckoned that he might have fourteen worn-out horses. The mobility that had always been one of his gang's great advantages was gone and even in his current state of semi-inebriation Lesley knew that he was in trouble.

Later that morning he received more bad news. Food supplies were running low. It had been easy enough to run off a few head of cattle for beef or to raid an isolated store for other food items, but that was when they had horses. He had a small army of gunmen but now would be unable to use most of them.

Murray Halloran was also in a foul mood. As the stubby outlaw strode around the camp his anxiety increased. He had brought his men into what was looking increasingly like a trap. He had never dreamed that Lesley was turning into a drunk and was appalled at the situation that had been allowed to develop. Every outlaw knew the importance of strong, reliable horses, except it seemed those who had been so smugly isolated in their own little world. The horses had been starved out of it and now it seemed that the men were facing a similar crisis. He would have to get Lesley off the whiskey long enough to form an emergency plan.

The telegraph lines would soon be open again and other lawmen would be coming in. Lesley's kingdom was doomed unless he could quickly resupply his force from the surrounding countryside. If his men had not lost all their horses, Halloran would have led them out, but it was too late. Cursing Lesley under his breath, the outlaw made his way to their leader's cave.

Lesley threw aside the empty bottle he was holding and walked out into the sunlight. He blinked in the bright light and focused his eyes on the stocky form striding purposefully toward him. In an attempt at humour he called, 'You're too late, Halloran. I just finished the last of the whiskey.'

'Good,' the other snapped. 'Now you can stop pickling your brain while we try to find a way out of this mess.'

★ ★ ★

Wolfe was tired. Over the last two days he had only managed a couple of hours' sleep. He had driven himself and those around him for he knew from experience the horror that would take place if Lesley's men got control of the town. Some resented taking orders from a man whose social standing had formerly been very low but fortunately a few could see that he was talking sense. Veile had appointed himself as his unofficial helper and the Hyles boy had proved another willing volunteer.

The new deputy was making progress. Slowly but surely his hesitant, nervous manner was going. He would argue now and spoke with the authority of one who knew the situation.

Wolfe was relieved when Delroy returned, hollow-eyed, hungry and suffering like he was from lack of sleep. The town might have been celebrating what they saw as a victory over King Lesley, but the deputy had no doubts that the main battle was yet to come

He was comparing notes with Delroy

when Rose walked into the office. She looked at them and said brightly, 'So you're safely home again, Marshal. You'll be pleased to know that Mort took good care of us while you were away. I must say though that you look a sorry pair. I hope that King Lesley doesn't attack us while you are half asleep like this. Both of you should be resting.'

'I can't, Rose,' Delroy argued. 'Lesley is likely to pay us a visit soon.'

Wolfe agreed. 'There's too much to do, Miss Allen. There's no time to rest.'

'Of course there is. Mister Veile will look after things for a couple of hours. He was in the Civil War and knows all about defending places.'

'Lesley was in the war, too,' Wolfe reminded her, 'and he knows all about attacking places.'

'No more arguments,' Rose said firmly. 'Both of you get some rest. I have been talking to Mr Veile and he is going to send out a few mounted volunteers so that we get plenty of warning. We know where to find you if we need you.'

Delroy looked at Wolfe with a tired smile on his lips. 'We'd better do as she says before she takes a switch to us, or at least makes us stand in the corner.'

For the first time in two years Wolfe laughed. He felt as though he was returning to a world that he had left.

14

Four hours later after a bath, a shave and a change of clothes, Delroy was attacking a meal in the hotel dining-room when Veile came in. He had been busy. He had sent out a few mounted volunteers to watch for any approach by Lesley's men and had taken another party out to repair the telegraph line. They had established contact with the operator at Belle Ridge and requested help from the local sheriff.

'That's a mighty good piece of work, Mr Veile,' the lawman said as he sawed at his steak. 'Sounds like you might have done this sort of thing before.'

The veteran looked around and, seeing that there was no one within earshot, he told Delroy, 'I don't want anyone to know this because I have a reputation to uphold. Can you keep a secret?'

'Whatever you say here goes no further.'

'During the war, I was once a major in the Union Army. My under-strength battalion was defending a small town in Kentucky when we were raided and forced out of it by rebel cavalry. It was a situation just like we have here. We were trying to hold too big an area with too few men. I wanted to meet them outside of town where we could concentrate our forces, but the colonel overruled me and tried to defend the town. Our men were pushed out with heavy losses both in men and supplies and our prestige took a battering. The colonel was a West Point man and had the right connections, but I didn't, having been promoted from the ranks. So you can guess who was blamed for the débâcle and cashiered. Later I rejoined the army under an assumed name as a private and had reached the dizzy heights of corporal when the war ended. I guess what I am trying to say is that I have seen this situation before. I know what can go wrong and know how to handle it.'

Delroy laid down his knife and fork. 'Well, that gives you an advantage over me. In my job we think half-a-dozen men is a big gang. I have never come up against a force the size of Lesley's. How would a soldier handle this situation?'

They talked for the next hour with Delroy supplying the information and the veteran calculating how to obtain the best advantage from it. Gradually a plan began to take place. They would meet Lesley's men outside of the town. Until the posse from Belle Ridge showed up, the numbers would be roughly equal, but the outlaws would have more experienced men and better weapons. Their weakness though would be their lack of mobility. The few horses Lesley's men possessed were frail and would not last long on a battlefield. By setting their main defences a mile or two out from the town, the Henly Springs men would force their enemies, who were mostly dismounted, to advance across an exhausting six miles of desert. If forced to retreat, the outlaws' canyon stronghold would prove to be their prison and starvation would do the rest. Both agreed that the looming battle would be a desperate one, but King Lesley could not avoid it. He would have to emerge from his kingdom and was doomed if he could not secure enough horses to make his escape.

'How much time do you reckon we have?' Delroy asked.

'If I was Lesley I'd be on my way tonight. His horses will be getting weaker by the hour. His men are not used to walking and it would be easier for them to travel by night than under the hot sun tomorrow.'

'So he has every reason to attack tonight?'

'He has — and here is another problem for us. Our men don't have the experience to fight them in the dark. I'm sure that with our strong horses we can hold them in daylight if everyone does as they are told, but we need to delay their attack until then.'

'How would you do it?'

'Most soldiers would send out a cavalry screen to detect any movement and delay the enemy until the main defences can be organized.

Delroy had an idea. 'What if I go out tonight with a couple of men and try to slow up any moves that Lesley might make? Could you and Mort Wolfe get the rest of our men together in a proper defensive position?'

'We could, if they will follow us. Civilians don't take orders like soldiers.'

The marshal stood up and pushed back his chair. 'Let's get our men together and talk to them. We might not have much time.'

★   ★   ★

Lesley's men were not happy when he gave them the news. They would be making a night march on Henly Springs and most of them would be dismounted. He shouted down the discontented mumblings pointing out that they had little alternative. They were extremely vulnerable until they could obtain fresh horses and the outlaws knew it.

Their three wounded men would have to remain in the canyon. One man with a slight leg wound would care for the other two until the gang came back. A couple of bandits were unhappy about that arrangement, but they had no option. After much arguing it was agreed that they would leave at 1 a.m. and would have plenty of time to get in position for a dawn attack. Halloran and Lesley would have a horse each, The others would be shared between the twelve lightest men in the band. Though initially there were a few objections, most outlaws agreed that the horses were vital to their success and had to be given every advantage.

'Drink up big, boys,' Halloran called to his men. 'There's no water between here and Henly Springs.'

Some outlaws had water canteens but others did not. Those on foot resented the extra weight of the water that they had to carry but realized that it might be worth its weight in gold if the battle proved to be a long one. Most were confident that they would meet little resistance from the townsfolk and were sure the desert march was their greatest challenge. A few were predicting that they would be into the town before they were detected.

Eventually all were assembled and the horsemen led them down into the main canyon that still reeked strongly with the smell of death.

★ ★ ★

Delroy and Crowley, with six other well-mounted and well-armed men, were making final plans with Veile. They would go out ahead of the force led by Wolfe and the veteran. If they encountered the bandits, and it was strongly suspected that they would, they would start harassing them and forcing the mounted outlaws to give chase. They would split into two groups of four men each hanging on the flanks of Lesley's force. If pressed hard one group would retreat while the other attacked the opposite side and lured the pursuit in that direction. It was important that Lesley's main force should be allowed to move straight ahead so it would run into the men that Veile had positioned in the centre.

Rose watched the preparations from the boardwalk near the sheriff's office. She was only too aware that plans could go wrong and reasoned that King Lesley had not survived for so long by being predictable. Delroy was standing a little apart from the others making a final adjustment to his saddle cinch so she walked across to where he was. 'You be careful out there tonight, Rod. I wouldn't like anything to happen to you.'

'I'll be careful,' he said, with a confidence that he did not really feel. 'Chances are that King Lesley won't come anyway. It's nice to know though that you are concerned about me.'

'I'm concerned about all these people here,' she said. 'Don't go thinking that you're anyone special.' Then Rose admitted softly, 'You might be just a little bit special.'

'Then how about a good luck kiss?'

'I usually save those for really special people,' she teased. 'But just this once I will promote you to a higher category.'

Delroy swept an arm around her and pulled her close. For a brief second his mouth met those soft lips, but then the voice of Crowley spoiled the moment.

'When you're finished saying good-bye, Marshal, me and the boys are ready to go.'

Rose gasped in embarrassment and stepped back while the lawman's romantic mood suddenly turned to thoughts of violence. But fortunately Crowley had turned his horse away, chuckling as he went.

'I'll be back as quick as I can,' Delroy promised, as he passed the reins around Duke's neck and stepped into the stirrup.

15

About twenty minutes riding from town they reached a dry creek bed where Veile decided to dismount his force. They would leave their horses both concealed and protected there with three men guarding them. The rest of the force followed the mounted group on foot for about a hundred yards and then, when they were sure that they would be directly in the raiders' path, they started digging in with tools they had brought from town. Some collected loose rocks to pile around their positions while others dug shallow pits in the softer ground and piled the displaced dirt in front of them. Strategically placed stones and uprooted bushes would conceal the positions until the bandits were close.

Veile strode about offering advice and encouragement. When finally satisfied at the siting of the position he walked over to where Delroy and his men were standing by their horses. Mindful that the enemy might have scouts in the area, he said softly, 'I need you men to give warning and delay Lesley for a while. Lure away his mounted men and try to run them around for as long as possible. Whatever you do, protect the flanks of my position. Stay close enough to give a hand if they reach my firing line. I don't know how well some of these men will stand. Above all, don't let any riders get around you to capture our horses, or worse, get into town.'

'Things will be a mite tricky in the dark,' the marshal told him, 'but we'll stick to your plan as much as we can. Frank will be on your right flank and I'll have my men on the left. Don't shoot us by mistake.' He turned to his men. 'Memorize the outline of those hills to the west so you will have some idea of where we are in the dark.'

Half a minute later, he said, 'Let's go,' and the mounted men rode out to find their enemies.

As close to the canyon's entrance as they dared to go, they spread out and waited.

Barely five minutes' march away, Halloran said to Lesley, 'It might be time to send a few scouts ahead, King. We don't want to walk into anything.'

Lesley scoffed at the idea. 'Those suckers in Henly Springs will be hiding inside their houses, or behind walls somewhere. I destroyed all their best fighting men.'

'Except those who run off our horses,' Halloran reminded.

'So what? They think that we'll sit back and try to get new horses before we raid the town. Come morning they're in for one hell of a shock.'

Then somewhere, not far ahead, a horse snorted.

Halloran reacted quickly. 'Someone's out there,' he whispered. 'Let's wait till the rest of the boys come up. I'll send forward a couple of men on foot just to see what we're up against.'

'There's no need,' Lesley said loudly. 'It could only be a couple of scouts. We'll soon chase them back to town.'

Delroy heard the voice and whispered to Crowley, 'Get them after us and then we'll split to each side. We want their horses to get plenty of work.' He stood in his stirrups and fired a shot into the blackness ahead.

The bullet did no damage, but Lesley spotted the muzzle flash. 'Come on,' he bellowed to his horsemen. 'We'll teach that sonofabitch to shoot at us.'

His riders needed to use their spurs and quirts to get their mounts into action but with wild yells, they charged after their leader.

Crowley threw a couple of shots in the outlaws' direction to keep them coming and then galloped to the side. To be sure he was followed, he fired another shot.

'He's over there,' a man shouted and the charging riders who saw the flash, changed direction.

The fresher, stronger horses of the

townsmen had no trouble leaving the pursuit behind.

'Time we took a hand,' Delroy told his men and they sent a volley of shots roughly in the direction of Lesley's riders.

'We're going the wrong way,' an outlaw called. 'They're behind us. Don't go chasing damn scouts.'

Hauling back on their reins, Lesley and his men first stopped and then turned their mounts. Halloran had not joined the rush and was firing at the gunflashes of Delroy's men. When the others galloped back he told them, 'I think most of them are on this side but there's not many of them. They don't seem too keen to fight.'

By this time the dismounted outlaws came toiling up. 'What's happening?' one man asked, as he panted for breath.

Lesley replied, 'They had a few scouts out. Just a few cowardly skunks skulking around in the dark. They can't hurt us. Let's push on toward the town. It's not long till daylight. I might have to go in first with the mounted men.'

'You have one less now,' a man growled. 'That bag of bones I've been riding, has just collapsed.'

'Now you have to walk like the rest of us,' a disgruntled outlaw said, unsympathetically.

Halloran was appalled at the situation he could see developing and suggested, 'We should ignore those riders out there. They can't hit us in the dark and we can hear them coming. If we keep an eye out on our flanks we can leave those clowns behind. They don't seem to want to stand and fight. It's no use running the guts out of the horses we have left; we need them for the first rush on the town.'

Out in the darkness Delroy sat still on his horse and listened. He could hear Lesley's men and noted with relief that they were moving in the direction of Veile's force. It was time to hit them again. He led his men out in an arc that he knew would take him behind the bandits and cut off their retreat to the canyon.

Crowley was keen to return to the fray but waited to see what action the marshal selected next. They had the outlaws at a disadvantage but that could change when day broke. When he heard the gunfire behind Lesley's men, he moved his group closer and dismounted them, leaving one man holding the horses, and opened up flanking fire on Lesley's left.

The outlaws were then in a dangerous crossfire, although because of the darkness it was not a particularly accurate fire. Bullets whistled overhead or whined away off rocks. Sooner or later one would have to strike living flesh.

'Keep moving forward,' Halloran called. He would use the protection that the darkness afforded. A daylight attack on Henly Springs would be a costly affair. It was better if they defeated the defence before their intended victims could see how few they really were.

Lesley knew that his mount had

154

almost reached the end of its strength and dismounted. For a small man, he was hard on horses, using a saddle designed mainly for rider comfort that threw his weight too far back on the horse. But now he was only too aware that he must save his mount all that he could. He hoped that it would have one final gallop in it when his men rushed the town. Halloran was already afoot leading his tall, bony sorrel gelding but a couple of outlaws remained mounted wheeling their horses about and firing from the saddle at those who were harassing them.

'Get off them horses, you danged fools,' Lesley bellowed. 'You're only wasting bullets and horse-flesh.'

Delroy smiled to himself when he heard Lesley's orders. They were confirmation that the outlaw horses were in desperate straits. Being directly behind the raiders, he had to be careful where he shot in case a stray bullet travelled through to where Veile was waiting. Even if it did no damage, a bullet might tempt one of their men to shoot back and ruin the ambush. Gathering his men around him, the lawman outlined his plan. Making plenty of noise they would dash at Lesley's men from behind hoping to drive them forward onto the waiting guns. But they needed to stop short before coming into too close a range because of the danger of the fire from Crowley's men.

'Make plenty of noise and fire a few shots but keep them low. We don't want stray slugs landing among Veile's men,' he told them.

They made their rush widely spaced and yelling like scalp-hunting Indians. Horseshoes struck sparks from the rocks and guns spat red flame in the outlaws' general direction. For a few seconds all was noise, gunflashes and powder smoke as both sides swapped ineffectual shots.

Then Delroy wheeled his horse away and his men followed.

King Lesley looked into the darkness

where the attackers had been. Finally his gaze turned to the east where the sun was making a red edge on the horizon. 'They think they're smart now,' he muttered to Halloran, 'but it will be light in half an hour and we'll see if they are game to take us on in the open.'

'Don't let them worry you too much, King. Henly Springs is not far ahead now and everything we need is in it. There's no point in going back to be trapped in the canyons. We need to go forward. It looks like we have to leave your kingdom behind.'

Lesley snarled, 'I ain't leaving nothing behind. I'm expanding my kingdom to take in Henly Springs.'

16

Wolfe licked his lips nervously as he crouched in a rifle pit and peered through the greasewood bush that screened the position. A couple of yards to his right and left others lay under cover peering into the gloom. Ahead in the darkness they heard shooting and saw the occasional muzzle flash. For two years he had waited for an opportunity to confront Lesley and now he found himself eagerly awaiting the coming battle. Until his funds had starting running low, the drifter had practised with rifle and six-gun and knew that he was a better than average shot. Because of the nervous tremor he had developed since his wife's murder, he had learned to shoot instinctively with his revolver as a natural extension of his hand. Where he pointed, the bullet would go. Now he would put all his practice to work.

He had only one fear as he waited: the fear that someone else would kill King Lesley before he did. Pictures of that morning two years ago were running through his mind. The scene seemed burned into his brain. Lesley was there holding a knife at Maryanne's throat and ordering him to drop his gun. He had complied in the vain hope that his wife's life might be spared. Both of them had been shot down and he considered himself the unfortunate one because he had lived. His revenge had been a long time coming but the day had finally arrived. Now he longed to see Lesley over the sights of a gun. He cared little what happened to him after that.

Veile moved quietly from one position to the next whispering instructions. The men were to hold their fire until he gave the order. Long-range shooting in bad light would do little damage to Lesley's men and could pose a risk to Delroy's men who were working closer to the raiders.

Day was breaking and indistinct shapes were revealed as trees and rocks and sometimes men. The townsmen could see a cloud of powder smoke and dust around Lesley's men. On the flanks they saw more dust as their horsemen raced about drawing the fire of the advancing outlaws but also herding them onto the waiting rifles

As the light improved, Delroy moved his men further from the bandits. There was no point in giving them easy targets. He hoped that on the other flank, Crowley was doing likewise. Their function was to keep Lesley's men moving on the same course and not to get involved in pitched battles that might force them into defensive positions short of the trap.

★　★　★

Rose had slept badly and it was still dark when she heard the shooting in the distance. She abandoned any ideas of sleep, climbed out of bed, listened for a while to the firing and dressed hurriedly. Begrudging the time it took, she forced herself to eat. Then she put on her wide-brimmed hat, picked up her father's medical bag and was about to leave the house when she remembered the little double-barrelled Remington derringer in the drawer of the sideboard. She took it out, checked that it was loaded and placed it in the side pocket of her dress.

A slight chill was still in the morning air, but the girl did not notice it as she hurried to Kopper's livery stable. To her surprise the old man was already dressed.

He pointed to the sound of the firing. 'So you heard it too?'

'I couldn't help but hear it. How far away is it?'

'Maybe a mile — two at the most.' Kopper narrowed his eyes and looked shrewdly at Rose. 'I suspect that this has something to do with your early morning visit.'

'It has. Men are probably being shot

out there and if they are, they need medical help urgently. My father always said that the quicker a doctor reached a badly injured person, the better their chances were.'

'And so you want me to go out there in the middle of a gunfight with a wagon picking up wounded men?'

'Something like that, Mr Kopper, except we should stay out of the fight. We don't help anyone by being killed, but I think we need the wagon just close enough for the wounded to reach it quickly. Will you help?'

'Looks like I have little choice. My wagon team work better for me than they do for anyone else and someone has to drive them. I might even take along my old Dragoon Colt. It's a bit out of date but there's nothing worse than needing a gun and not having one.'

'Thank you, Mr Kopper.

'Don't thank me yet, girlie. This day's a long way short of being over. One or both of us could finish up regretting this idea.'

Things went wrong just as it was full daylight. Nobody was sure who fired the shot. It might even have been an accidental discharge, but a rifle shot came from the hidden townsmen and alerted Lesley to the fact that not all his enemies were hanging about the flanks of his force.

'There's someone ahead,' Halloran called. 'We could be boxed in.'

Another bandit who had ridden his horse onto a piece of higher ground called out, 'I can see horses in that arroyo ahead. They must be waiting for us on foot.'

There was no going back and Lesley knew it. 'Let's not disappoint the bastards. We are going straight through and we'll take those fresh horses as we go. Don't be scared of a few old shopkeepers.'

Both he and Halloran mounted for what they knew to be a do-or-die effort. Neither would have chosen such a situation but suddenly they had run out of options.

'Get through to those horses,' Halloran called as he set spurs to his mount. 'We must get those horses.'

Even the most cowardly of the outlaws knew that their best chance of escaping was a frontal attack. The mounted ones kicked their weary horses in to a canter and the men on foot ran after them. Some shouted in defiance as they came but most had little breath to spare and advanced in grim silence.

A nervous townsman took one look at the force bearing down on them and opened fire without waiting for Veile's order. The range was too long for some of the more indifferent shots but that did not stop them from firing. A roar went up from the attackers when they realized that they charged through the first irregular volley with no loss.

A horse staggered and went down but it was the combination of exhaustion and rough ground that caused the fall. The rider jumped clear, rolled to his feet and continued to rush forward. Here and there a man paused and fired at the defensive positions ahead but most just ran forward eager to come to grips with their opponents.

Delroy was quick to realize the threat against the main force. 'They're over-running Veile,' he called as he wheeled Duke to the right. 'Come on.'

The bay horse sprung into a gallop. His rider pointed him in the right direction and then left it to his mount to cover the rough ground the best way that it could.

'Keep firing,' Veile shouted. 'Don't let them past.' He stood upright in his rifle pit and threw a shot at the nearest rider. But he did not live to see the result of his effort. A bullet came from somewhere among the attackers and hit him in the centre of the forehead.

Wolfe was frantically firing and reloading but had the demoralizing feeling that his shots were bringing no execution. Men were coming and going in a cloud of gun smoke and red dust kicked up by the horses. And that cloud was rolling closer by the second. He was seeking Lesley, but in the confusion failed to find him. A horse loomed above him and the drifter fired up at its rider but the man was still in the saddle as the animal bounded past. He was through their defences and riding hard for the horses being held behind the firing line.

Another horse, its strength almost gone, came staggering between the rifle pits while its rider fired from the saddle. Behind him an outlaw emerged from the dust, jumped to the ground and charged Wolfe firing as he came. The drifter's carbine clicked empty and he drew his revolver just as a bullet tugged at his sleeve. Wolfe's return shot took the running man in the chest and he crashed backwards.

Lesley's mount was already failing when, a few yards short of the townsmen's line, it took a bullet in the brain and dropped instantly. The outlaw leader crashed down with his mount and struck his head on a rock as he landed. Unconscious, he did not see his men rushing past him.

More dismounted bandits had arrived by then and total chaos ensued as men shot and struck at each other in frantic attempts to survive. Some bandits paid little attention to the defenders after they had broken through them. They only had eyes for the horses they could see in the nearby creek bed.

The three guarding the horses saw that Lesley's men had broken through and were charging toward them. They dropped the reins they were holding as they prepared to fight for their lives. Some horses stood but others scattered.

17

The horse holders stared in horror at the apparently unstoppable gunmen bearing down on them. Then one came out of his shock enough to start firing. One of the attackers stumbled, but then roared with anger and came on again.

It was at this point that Delroy and his men burst upon the scene. Risking a bullet from one of the nervous guards, the marshal charged across the front of the position in a desperate bid to intercept the gunmen who had by-passed the main line of defence. The only mounted outlaw who had penetrated that far had almost reached the creek bed when he saw the lawman charging in from the side. He tried to turn his mount to face the new threat but the animal was so weak and its movements so sluggish that it had only half turned when Duke cannoned into it. The horse was thrown violently on its side and the force of the collision catapulted the rider some yards from his mount. The gun in his hand went flying and a defender shot him before he could even begin to look for it.

The three men who rode with Delroy arrived then and placed themselves between the defensive line and the creek bed. Through the swirls of dust Crowley's men arrived from the other flank. They too had seen the danger and had hastened to retrieve the situation. Then the horsemen combined and advanced through the swirling dust to where Wolfe and the others were fighting for their lives. With their arrival, the fight went out of the bandits and they scattered.

Always cool in a crisis, Halloran retreated around the northern end of the townsmen's defence. He saw that some of the horses had broken loose from where they had been concealed. The animal he rode had been killed early in the fighting. If he could catch one of those, he would have a slender chance of escaping. He did not know where Lesley was, nor did he care. He blamed the self-appointed king for their current situation. The firing had dwindled to the odd, distant shot and men were emerging warily from cover seeking companions among the casualties.

Delroy sighted a loose horse, obviously an old rogue trotting away with its head held sideways so as to avoid treading on the trailing reins. Someone will need that horse later, he told himself and steered Duke on a course that would intercept it. He was not the only one watching the horse. Halloran, on his hands and knees in a clump of mesquite, watched the animal approaching. He could not break cover suddenly without frightening it, but he would surely be seen if he walked quietly out into the open. Then he saw a rider on a blaze-faced bay cantering in his direction. If he shot that man out of his saddle, he would have the choice of two horses.

Delroy was concentrating on the loose horse and, as he turned Duke around it, he saw a flash of movement out of the corner of his eye. He turned his head and found himself looking into the muzzle of Halloran's gun. His own was still in his hand, but the outlaw was at his left rear, the most difficult place for a mounted man to defend. The range was short and a miss would be most unlikely.

Click. The hammer fell on a spent cartridge. In the confusion Halloran had not been counting his shots. But to a degree the speed of his reaction almost compensated for his oversight. He hurled the empty gun in the lawman's face as the latter swung his horse around. Then he snatched a smaller weapon from his belt.

The outlaw's aim was good and the thrown revolver struck Delroy above the left eye with considerable force. The latter reeled under the impact, but did not fall from his mount. Almost as a reflex action he fired as Halloran brought up his gun. The bullet caught the stocky outlaw in the face and he flew backwards to land flat on his back on the ground. He twitched slightly so the marshal took no chances and fired another shot into the fallen man's chest. Then he reloaded his gun, caught the loose horse and returned it to where the shaken guards were collecting their charges again. He felt blood trickling down his face from a cut over his eye but knew that the injury was not serious.

The area was littered with dead and wounded men and dead horses, and the townsmen were still recovering from the shock of the furious assault by the desperate outlaws. Instead of pursuing their beaten enemies they were looking for friends and tending to their wounded. None felt like continuing the fight.

Wolfe had survived and reloaded his Winchester as he began prowling the battlefield looking for Lesley. He had not seen him during the fighting.

'It's not over yet,' Delroy called, as he saw a couple of outlaws fleeing back toward the canyon. He paused only long enough to wipe the blood out of his eye with his sleeve and then galloped off in pursuit. Crowley and two other riders went with him. The rearmost fugitive turned and lifted his gun, but then realized the futility of his action. Letting the weapon drop, he raised his hands.

'Are we taking prisoners today?' Crowley asked, as he readied his carbine expectantly.

'We are,' the marshal said firmly, 'but watch for tricks.'

All the fight had gone out of the bandit. The long march, the fight and the day's heat had all taken their toll. He stood there hoping that he would not be shot out of hand. 'Don't shoot,' he pleaded. 'I surrender.'

'Look after him, Frank,' Delroy ordered. 'The rest of us will collect a few more.'

'Why worry about the others, Marshal? You should do something about that eye. If a handful of survivors get back to the canyon they have nowhere to go. We can get them later. Besides' — he pointed — 'look who's just arrived.'

Delroy turned to see Kopper's wagon approaching and he saw the girl in the blue dress seated beside the driver.

'Me and the boys will keep after any of these skunks that are left. You go and get that wound seen to. You're bleeding like a stuck pig,' Crowley told him. Then, with a sly smile on his face, he said, 'Who knows? Someone might even kiss you hello like she kissed you goodbye.'

'One of these days I'm going to murder you,' Delroy threatened, as his tormentor rode away laughing.

The dry river-bed stopped the wagon from coming any closer but Rose, clutching her medical bag, jumped down from the seat. Wolfe went to meet her. There was no time for small talk.

'How many wounded?' Rose asked, as she looked across the battleground.

'At least three of our own and possibly some of Lesley's men could still be lying out there in the brush. We have three dead too.'

'Who's the worst hurt?'

'I don't know for sure but Ed Page is hit pretty bad. That's him over there near that dead horse.'

As she hurried across to the wounded man, Rose looked up to see the marshal riding toward her. His face and shirt were bloody but, to her relief, his movements were not those of a badly injured man. Though relieved, she put her personal feelings aside and went to work on the wounded man before her.

Delroy dismounted and led Duke across to where Kopper waited with the wagon. 'You took a hell of a risk coming out here,' he said sternly. 'For a while there it looked like we would lose this fight.'

'But you didn't and Miss Rose was right. The quicker them wounded get attention the better their chances are. You look like you had a near thing yourself. What happened?'

'One of Lesley's pistoleros threw a gun at me. He had tried to shoot me with it but found it was empty. I shot him before he could get his other gun into action.'

'Have we lost many men?'

'Three that I know of. One was Veile.'

Kopper shook his head and said sadly, 'He was one of the best. Henly Springs could not afford to lose a man like that.'

'I won't argue with you there,' Delroy said quietly.

Before the lawman could say more, he saw Crowley and his companions riding back slowly herding a dismounted and unarmed bandit ahead of them.

'Is he the last of them?' Delroy called.

The cowhand halted his horse and dismounted. 'There could be another couple but we can get them later. We had to shoot one other owlhoot who was wounded, but didn't have sense enough to surrender. Our horses are just about done up, but we might need them again soon by the look of things.'

'Why's that?'

Crowley pointed. 'Look behind you.'

Delroy and Kopper turned to see a cloud of dust rapidly approaching and below the dust they could see riders.

18

'Riders coming,' Delroy called. 'We need a few rifles over here. A couple of you help Miss Allen get the wounded into the creek bed.'

Their recent bloody experience had taught the townsmen much and now they needed no urging to move smartly into defensive positions. Anxiously they watched the riders approach.

'It could be the help we called for from Belle Ridge,' the lawman said as he peered at the new arrivals. 'But we can't let ourselves be taken by surprise if they are reinforcements for Lesley's men.'

'How close do we let them come before we fire?' a man called.

'Nobody fire until I give the word. That could be the posse from Belle Ridge.'

Kopper quickly solved the riddle of

the newcomers' identity. 'It's Mark Simmons, the sheriff of Belle Ridge. I sold him that big pinto horse he's riding. You don't often see pintos that big. That's Simmons for sure. I can recognize that high-crowned brown hat he always wears too.'

'Nobody fire,' Delroy shouted. 'They're friendly.'

Mark Simmons was tall and powerfully built. He halted his big horse and surveyed the scene as Delroy approached. A look of disappointment showed briefly on his broad face. 'Looks like we got here too late,'

The marshal introduced himself and assured him that there was likely to be plenty of action still to come. He told the sheriff, 'We know that a couple of Lesley's crowd are making their way back to the canyons and others might be hiding out around here in the brush. Our men and horses are pretty close to exhaustion and we have a few wounded here.'

'My posse will follow up those who

are trying to get back to the canyons,' Simmons volunteered. 'I'll send a rider back to you if we strike anything we can't handle.'

'I should warn you that things won't be pretty in the main canyon. Lesley ambushed Sheriff Henderson's posse in there about a week ago. They are still lying there. Some of the Henly Springs men will need to identify them too.'

The sheriff shifted his weight in the saddle. He was keen to get moving. 'I'll go after the others now,' he said. 'Give your men an hour or two of rest and let any who want to, join us then. Meanwhile, I suggest you get your wounded back to where they can get proper care.' He added, 'It looks like you could do with some yourself.'

'I'll survive,' Delroy told him. 'Be careful. King Lesley must still be in there somewhere.'

But Delroy's assumption was wrong.

The outlaw leader was not far away concealed in a patch of tall weeds. Covered in blood from the horse, he looked like a dead man to any who had time to notice in the confusion of the battle. Consequently he attracted little attention at first. The main fight was over when he recovered consciousness. Instinct told him to remain still. As his aching head slowly cleared, Lesley knew that he was in trouble. His guns were gone. He remembered dropping one when it was empty, but had no idea where the other one was. It might have been under his dead horse, but he certainly had no chance to go looking for it. Men were walking about and there was no shooting. His attack had failed.

Peering from beneath the brim of his hat, he chanced his first move while his enemies were watching the arrival of the wagon. He rolled into a nearby shallow ditch and lay still. The arrival of the Belle Ridge posse was another distraction and he crawled a few more yards to where the high weeds offered better protection. But no better hiding place was available. Here he would have to remain until the others left or the chance of seizing a horse presented itself.

Wolfe watched Simmons and his men ride away. He was uneasy that nobody had seen Lesley in the fight and suspected that he had been among those who retreated to the canyon. To his surprise the desire for revenge had diminished and he felt that helping with the wounded was more important. After two years of hoping to confront the man who had ruined his life, he suddenly found that he had other priorities. As long as Lesley was killed or captured, he no longer felt the need for personal involvement.

Rose was working with calm efficiency, stopping bleeding, bandaging and splinting broken limbs. Her white apron was covered in bloodstains and there was little water to clean wounds. She had brushed the hair back from her face and left a bloody mark on her forehead as she finished the bandage on the last patient. 'Mr Wolfe,' she said,

'Could you get some men and transfer these wounded men to the wagon? We need to get them back to town.' Then she saw Delroy standing nearby. 'Come over here, Rod, and let me see that eye.'

The marshal walked across and sat on the ground beside her. His eye was swelling shut.

Gently she wiped away some of the blood and exposed the wound. 'That will need a stitch or two. I'll put them in while the wounded are being loaded into the wagon. I'm afraid I have nothing to deaden the pain so feel free to yell if it hurts.'

It did hurt. Much as he tried to show indifference to pain, Delroy drew in his breath and grunted as the stitch went in and was drawn tight.

'I'm sorry to hurt you,' Rose said gently as she felt him flinch, 'but it can't be helped. Just hold still and it will soon be over.'

Delroy gritted his teeth and a cold sweat came out on his forehead. 'Don't worry, just get it done.'

The second stitch was as painful as the first but then Rose snipped off the loose ends, stood up and said brightly, 'It's all over now. You were very good. My father would always give candy to the children he had to stitch but I guess you are a bit old for that — and we don't seem to have any candy anyway.'

'Maybe you could kiss it and make it better.

Rose laughed. 'You need at least four stitches for that. Now make yourself useful and help get our other patients comfortable so we can send them back to town.'

'Are you going with them?'

'I'm not sure. There might be other wounded men before all this is over. There have been a few shots since Sheriff Simmons left us. If there is a spare horse I might pack up my kit and go to the canyon with our men.'

Delroy looked grave. 'You won't like what you find in that canyon. I think you should go back with the wagon.'

'I've seen dead people before, Rod.'

'Not like these will be. However, if you insist on going I'll get a horse for you. Unfortunately we have plenty of spare ones.'

They decided to leave the dead where they were until all the wounded had been returned to town. Wolfe and a couple of helpers carried in the bodies of the three dead townsmen and covered them with blankets from the wagon.

Delroy selected a horse for Rose, emptied the contents of the saddle-bags into the wagon and replaced them with her medical supplies.

Two elderly townsmen were nearing the point of exhaustion and at Rose's suggestion, they would ride back with the wagon leading the spare horses. Once there they undertook to organize other wagons to come out from Henly Springs to collect the bodies. They would also telegraph Belle Ridge requesting the services of the town doctor.

Finally Kopper swung his team about

and the little procession. started back for Henly Springs.

Rose, Wolfe and the marshal were left standing by their horses listening for gunshots that might come from the canyon.

'We might as well get going,' Delroy suggested. 'Nothing else is going to happen around here until the wagons get back.'

He was wrong.

19

Lesley could not believe his luck. Suddenly most of his enemies were gone. Only two men and a woman remained. They had guns and horses and the outlaw was confident that he would soon be able to acquire both.

He reached into his boot top and withdrew the short-bladed, razor-sharp knife from its special sheath. He knew he would have to move like lightning and his muscles tensed like those of a rattlesnake about to strike. But there could be no warning rattle.

To a degree, Rose played into Lesley's hands. Finding her horse a bit tall, she led it to a patch of uneven ground so that she could mount from the high side. The horse was between her and the two men when Lesley made his move.

He bounded across the few feet separating them and seized the startled girl from behind. She screamed in alarm as an arm encircled her and she felt the point of a knife at her throat.

Delroy and Wolfe turned to see Rose's startled face showing over the back of her horse and Lesley holding her at knife point.

'Drop your guns — I'll kill her if you don't.'

The marshal saw that there was little he could do and was about to unbuckle his gunbelt but Wolfe had seen this situation before.

'Don't drop your gun, Marshal. He'll kill us all anyway. I fell for this once before.'

If recognition dawned on Lesley, he did not show it. 'I'll kill her if you don't,' he threatened. 'I only want a horse and a gun. If I get them I'll let you go.' He tightened the grip around Rose's neck and demanded, 'Tell them, lady, because if I have to die I'm going to cut your throat as I go.'

'You're choking me,' Rose gasped. She was playing for time. While Lesley was closely watching the two armed men, he did not see her slip her hand into her pocket. As her fingers closed around the derringer's small butt, she spoke loudly to cover the sound of the hammer being cocked. 'Let me go.'

'Not a chance,' Lesley chuckled. He had exploited similar situations before and was living proof that his tactics were effective.

Pointing the weapon backwards, Rose took a deep breath and fired through her dress pocket.

Lesley jerked upright in surprise at the report of the little gun and the heat of the bullet grazing his thigh. The split-second distraction was enough.

Wolfe drew and fired. The bullet went over Rose's shoulder and took the outlaw through the right eye. He collapsed instantly and almost dragged the girl down with him.

For one horrified instant Delroy thought Rose might have been shot, but then he saw her roll away from Lesley's corpse.

Wolfe walked forward as smoke still floated from the barrel of his gun. There would be no need for a second shot.

'You could have shot Rose,' the marshal accused.

Wolfe gave a grim smile. 'I knew what I was doing. I have practised that shot so many times that I could just about do it in my sleep. A man's head at ten feet is a pretty big target. Lesley killed my wife in a situation like this and he nearly killed me. I was not going to let it happen again.'

Delroy helped Rose to her feet. She was pale but determined to continue her mission. She smiled at Wolfe. 'Thank you, Mort. You saved my life.' Then she noticed that her dress was scorched and smouldering from the derringer's discharge.

Delroy saw it and beat the area with his hat to stop it bursting into flames.

'A fine lawman you are,' a mocking voice came from behind him. 'The rest of us are fighting outlaws and you wait behind beating up women.'

Delroy turned to see that Crowley had ridden back to them. 'One of these days — ' he threatened.

The cowhand laughed. 'I was on my way back to get Miss Rose here. There's a wounded outlaw might need some help.' He nodded toward Wolfe. 'That was mighty fancy shooting, Mort. I saw it as I rode up.'

'I'm afraid I wasn't much help,' Delroy said apologetically. 'I would never have dared try a shot like that.'

'Most men wouldn't,' Wolfe told him. 'That's what he was counting on. It's a trick he used on me, so he knew it had worked before. He would have killed all three of us if he had been able to get a gun.'

The marshal caught Rose's horse and led it across to her. 'If you feel up to it, we can see how Sheriff Simmons is doing.'

She mounted her horse, glanced at the sprawled remains of King Lesley and said, 'Lead on.'

20

The next three days were busy ones as the citizens of Henly Springs gathered their dead and the funerals began.

Sheriff Simmons and his posse had scoured the canyons that Lesley had called his kingdom. They killed another bandit and brought in three wounded ones. It was Simmons who found the body of Campbell, the scout who had guided the ill-fated posse. 'Lesley's men got him quick with a club of some kind,' he explained. 'I guess he was the first one killed. I know that survivors claimed to see him much further into the canyon, but I think that was someone riding his horse and impersonating him, just to lead them further into the trap.'

The arrival of the doctor from Belle Ridge had saved Rose from total exhaustion, but there had still been a harrowing round of funerals before she could really rest.

Delroy's boss had sent him a telegraph message. It was time for him to move on. The gist of the message was that as Sheriff Simmons had rid the town of King Lesley, there was no need for a federal officer to be there.

Mort Wolfe was outraged when he heard that Delroy had been given no recognition for his efforts. As the man who killed King Lesley, Wolfe had been elected sheriff. Rose and Kopper would be remembered for their parts, but Frank Crowley and the marshal were already forgotten men.

The cowhand had left town quietly and the sorrel mare that had caught his eye was found to be missing. from among the captured horses. Nobody begrudged him the horse. Crowley had played his part well but asked for nothing in return.

Delroy's left eye was still black and swollen as he packed his mule prior to his departure. Rose had been sleeping when he received his orders and though he wanted to, he did not feel that he should disturb her well-earned rest. The evening before, he had slipped a note under the front door of her home but feared that she might have missed it when she walked into the unlit house.

Finally, he could delay no longer. He made a last unnecessary adjustment to the pack, took Duke's reins and shook hands with Wolfe. 'Will you say goodbye to Rose for me?'

The new sheriff smiled and looked over Delroy's shoulder. 'No need. You can do it yourself.'

Following Wolfe's gaze he saw Rose hurrying toward him and to his mind she had never looked more beautiful.

'You were leaving without saying goodbye, Rod,'

'I didn't like to disturb you, Rose. You were worn out. I was hoping that I'd see you though. I'd like to stay but I can't. There's been a mail robbery over near the Colorado border and I have to go.'

'Will you be back this way soon?'

The marshal smiled. 'Will I be a bit more special if I come back?'

'Maybe just a little bit.'

Ignoring the other people on the street, Delroy took her in his arms and kissed her. 'I'll be back,' he promised.

GOLD FOR DURANGO

Carlton Youngblood

When James Buckley Armstrong comes upon a young woman fighting off two men, he finds that his deadly .44 Colt changes their minds. But then Rufus Ludel, her husband, rides up with his men, and he wants Buck hanged. He escapes the necktie party, only to run headlong into a range war and a series of gold bullion robberies. Buck tries to help with the gold shipment but is mistrusted by everyone it seems . . . including the local vigilante committee.

THE DUEL AT MURPHY'S FORD

Tom Benson

Eli Riley is the marshal of Murphy's Ford, a copper mining town. But when the town's water supply is poisoned, the copper company is blamed. Then trouble starts: two prominent citizens are killed and a stranger arrives looking to avenge their deaths. Murphy's Ford is divided, and a vigilante mob heads for the mine owners. Eli, involved in a shoot-out as the water poisoners become known, faces a growing demand for their lynching. How would it all end?

TOUGH JUSTICE

Skeeter Dodds

When Ike Durrel robs the bank at Arrow Bend and kidnaps the banker's daughter, Jack Lane is unexpectedly thrown a lifeline to survival after he'd faced certain death. Despite the probability of failure against the outlaw Durrel, it's the only way out of Jack's financial trouble. Faced with an uprising in Indian country, and Ike Durrel and his brother, Ned, he must rescue Emily Watts. Surprisingly, Lane's mission is almost completed — until he is suddenly pitched into deadly danger . . .

HELL'S COURTYARD

Cobra Sunman

Indian Territory, popularly called Hell's Courtyard, was where bad men fled to escape the law. Buck Rogan, a deputy marshal hunting the killer Jed Calder, found the trail leading into Hell's Courtyard and went after his quarry, finding every man's hand against him. Rogan was also searching for the hideout of Jake Yaris, an outlaw running most of the lawlessness directed at Kansas and Arkansas. Single-minded and capable, Rogan would fight the bad men to the last desperate shot.

SARATOGA

Jim Lawless

Pinkerton operative Temple Bywater arrives in Saratoga, Wyoming facing a mystery: who murdered Senator Andrew Stone? Was it his successor, Nathan Wedge? Or were lawyers Forrest and Millard Jackson, and Marshal Tom Gaines involved? Bywater, along with his sidekick Clarence Sugg, and Texas Jack Logan, faces gunmen whose allegiances are unknown. The showdown comes in Saratoga. Will he come out on top in a bloody gun fight against an adversary who is not only tough, but also completely unforeseen?